MARGRET & H.A. REY'S
IN Curious George® SUPER GEORGE!

Houghton Mifflin Harcourt

Boston   New York

www.hmhco.com

Written by Liza Charlesworth
Illustrations by Fran Brylewska and David Brylewski
for Artful Doodlers Ltd.

ISBN: 978-1-328-73623-9

Manufactured in China
SCP 10 9 8 7 6 5 4 3 2 1
4500702595

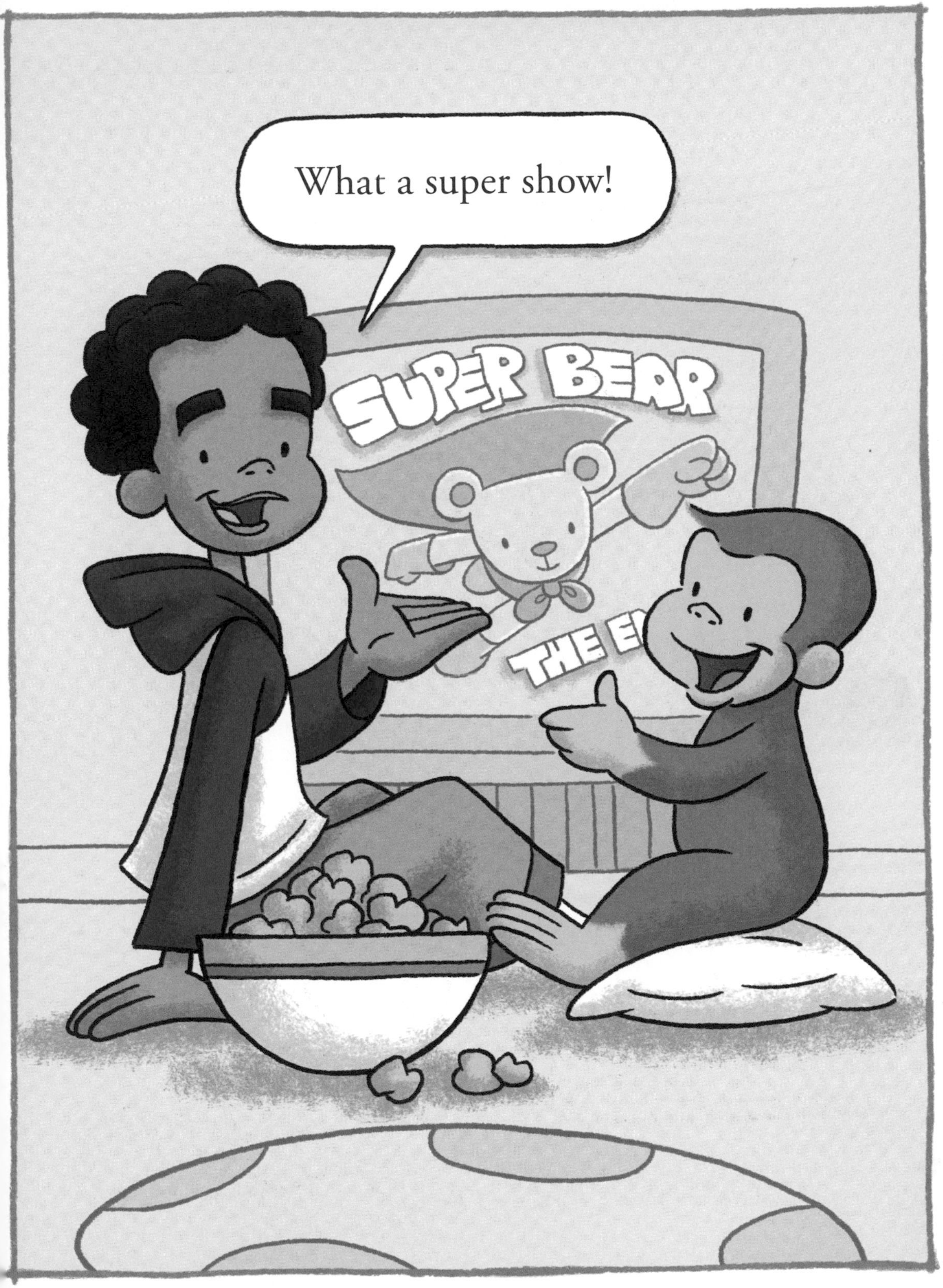
What a super show!
SUPER BEAR

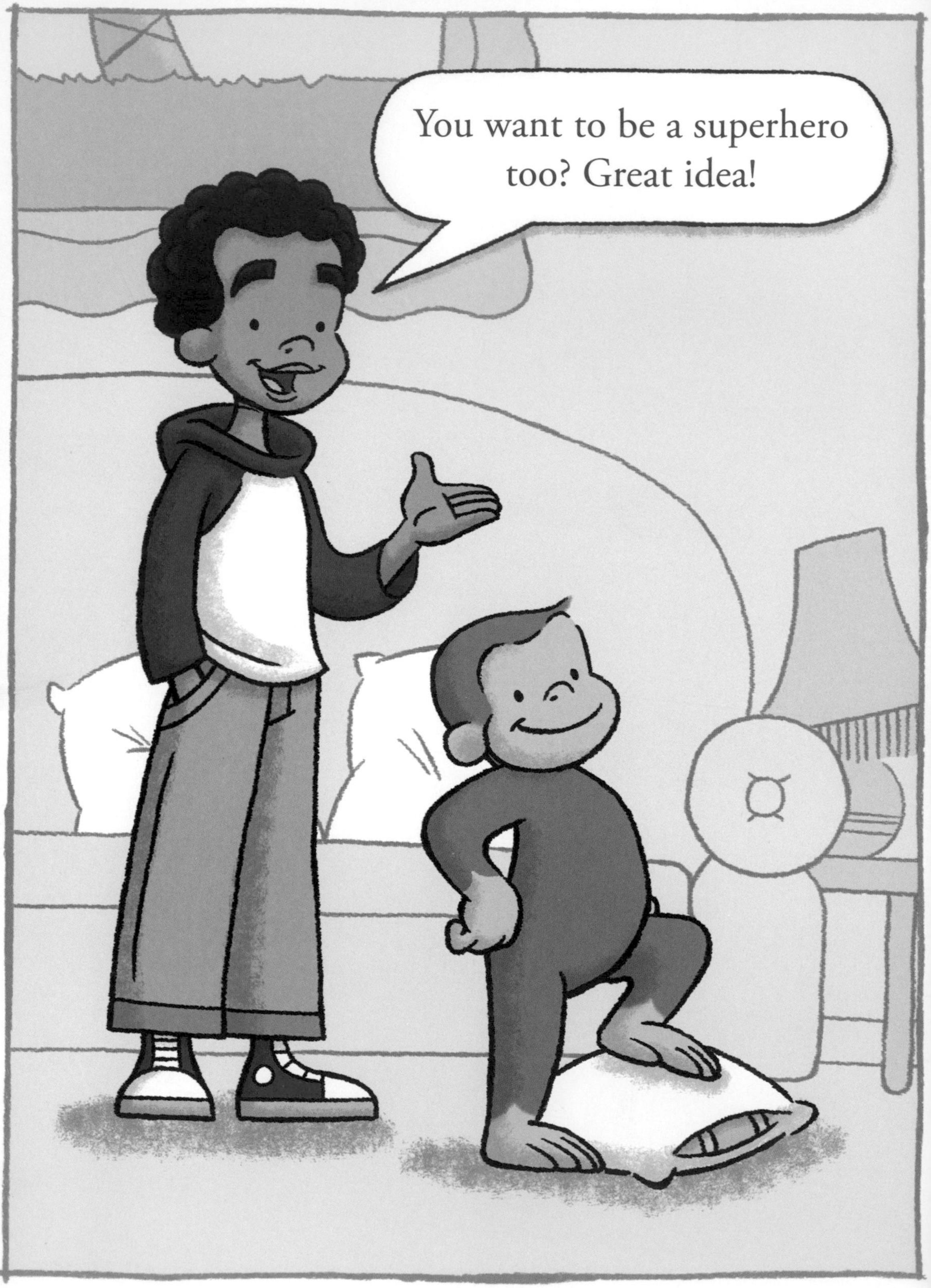
You want to be a superhero too? Great idea!

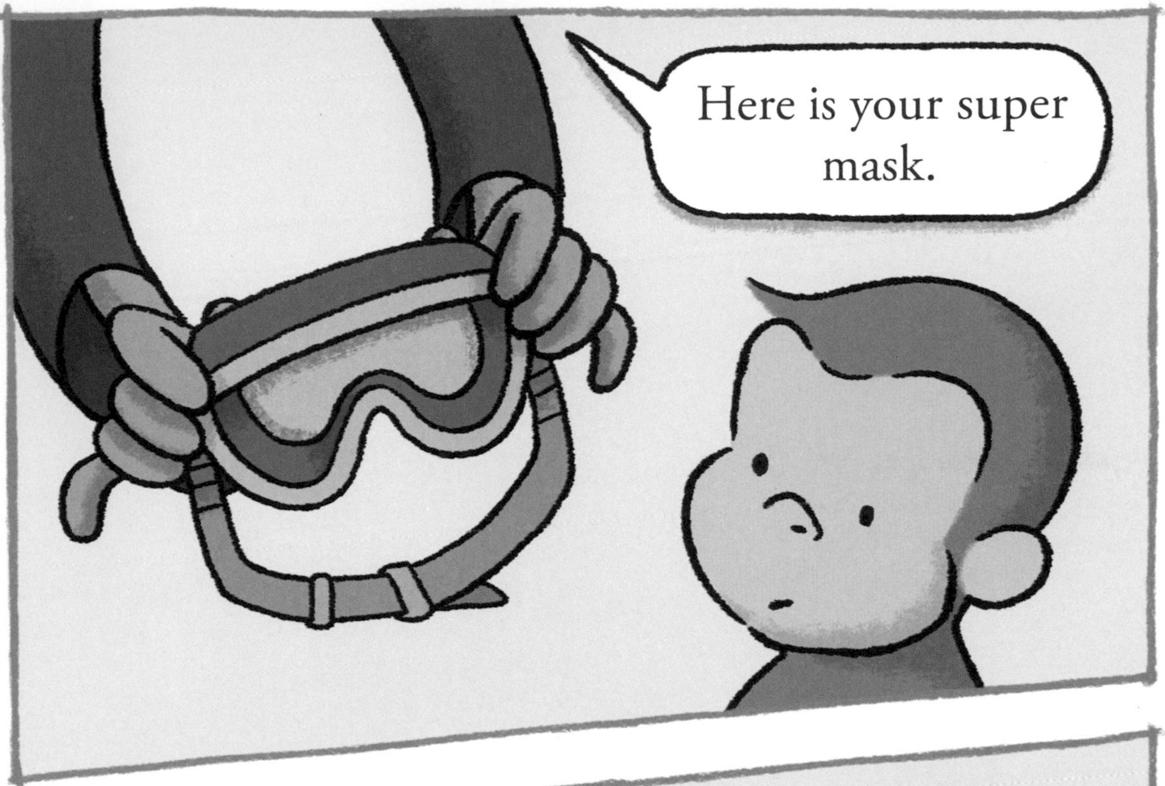
Here is your super mask.

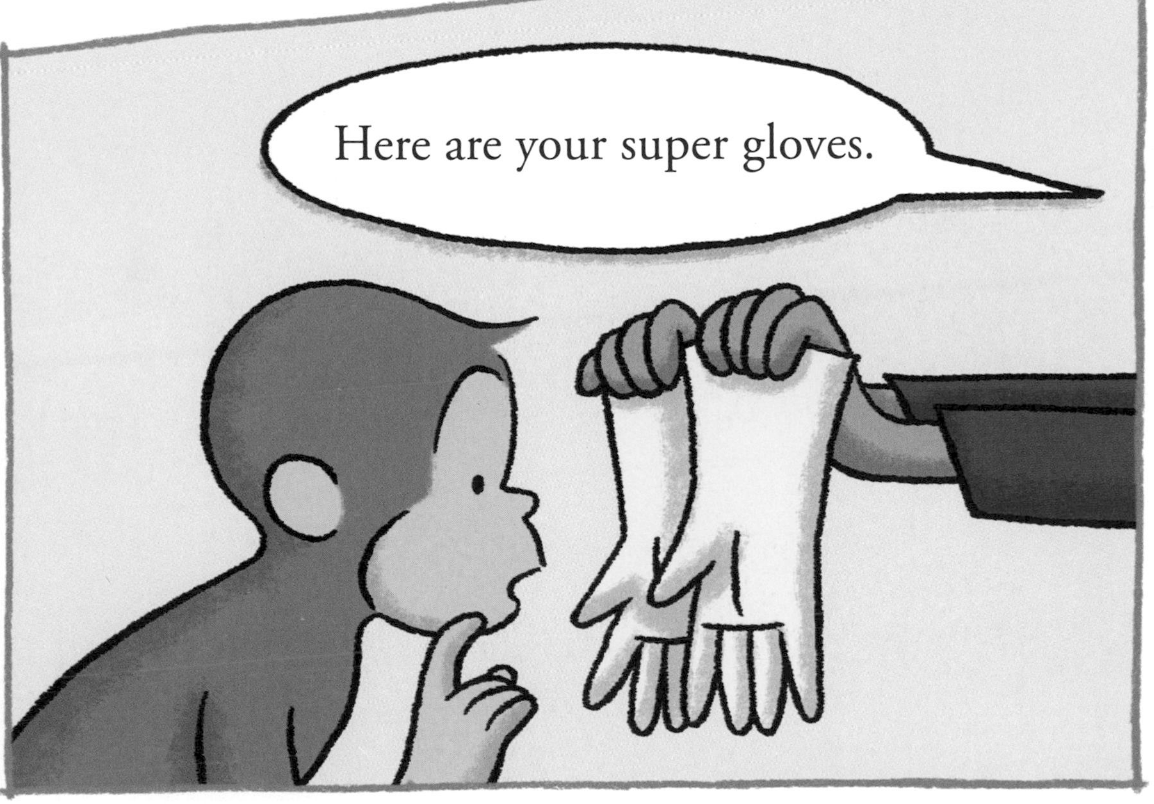
Here are your super gloves.

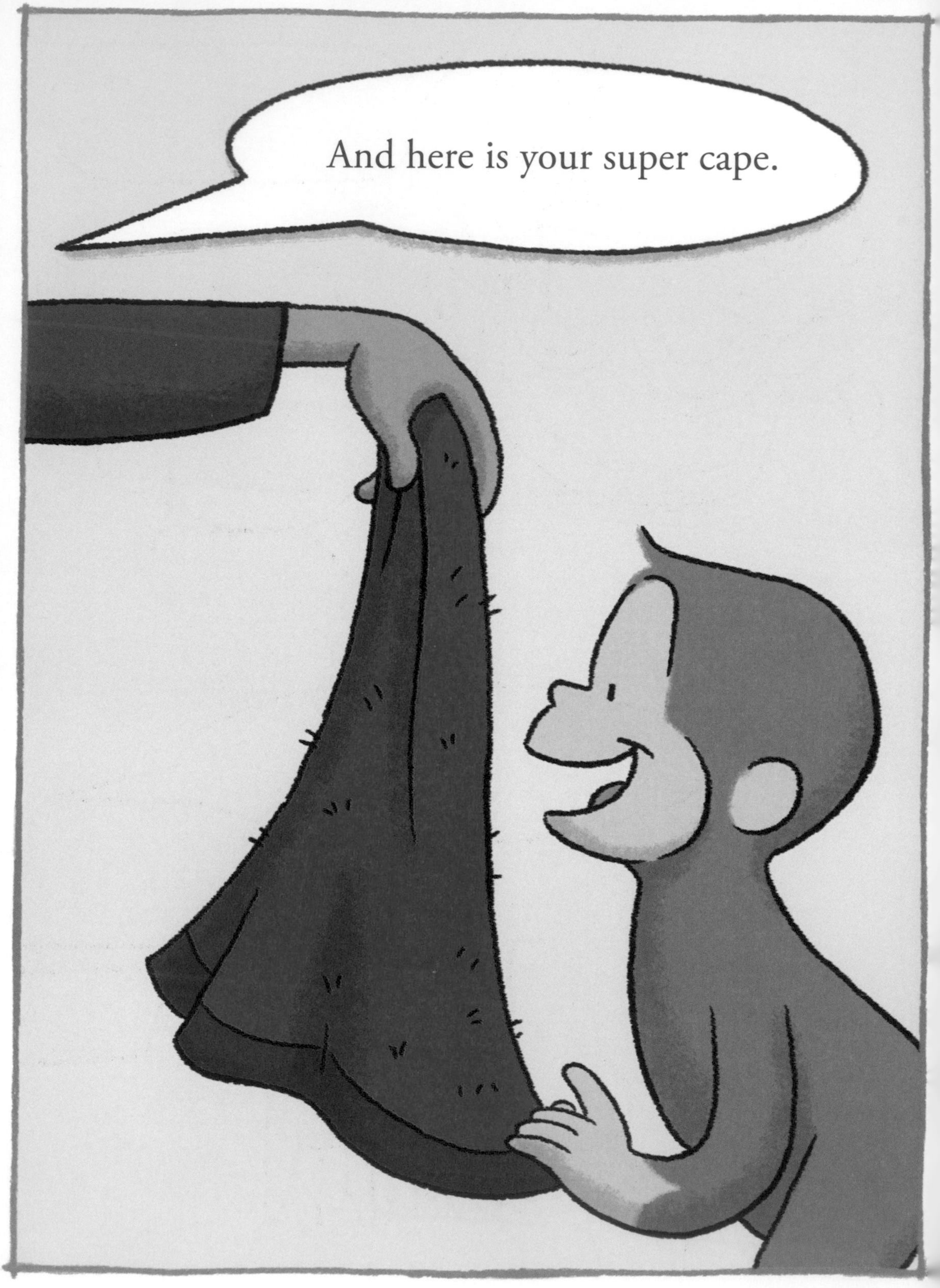
And here is your super cape.

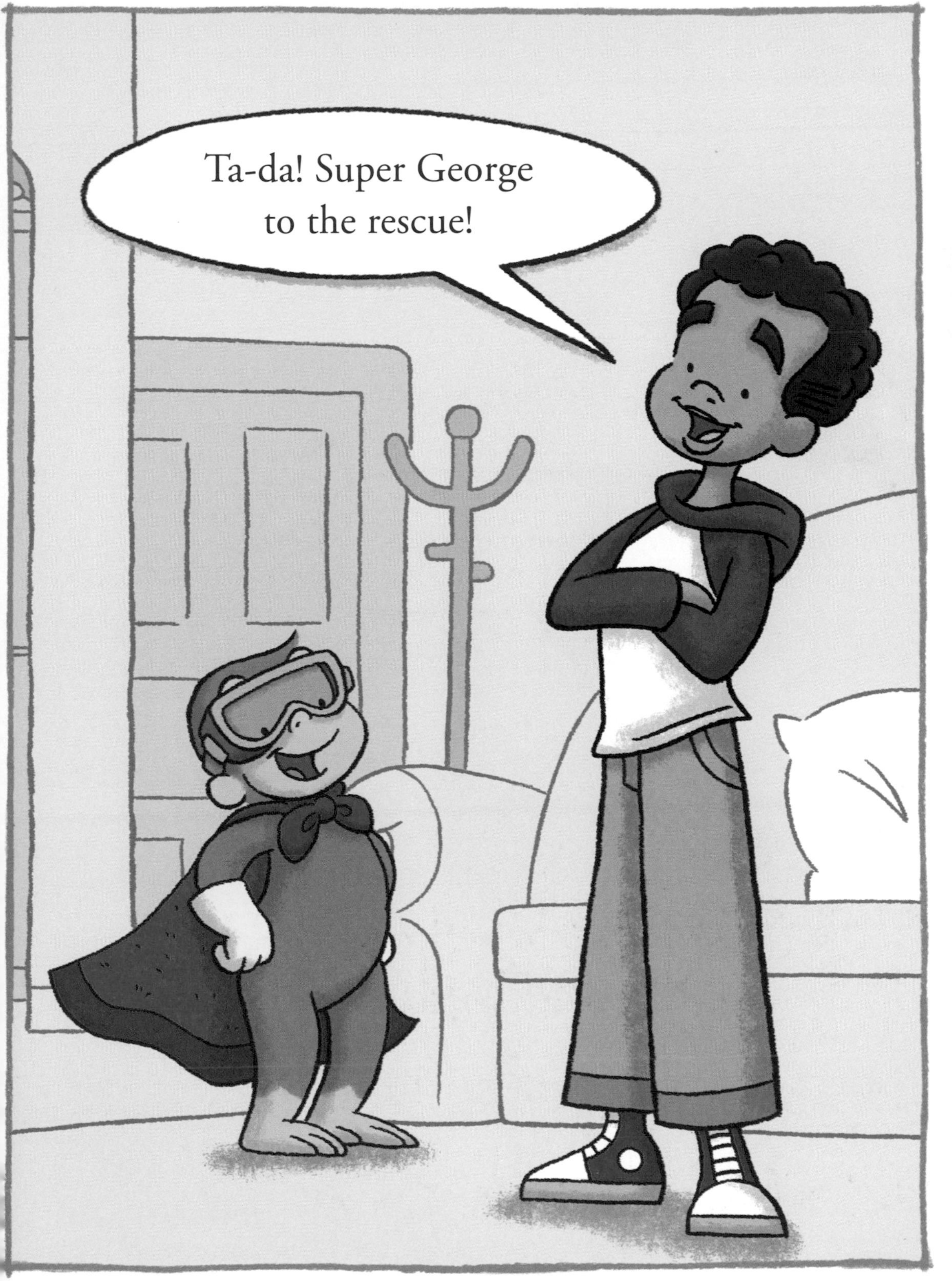
Ta-da! Super George to the rescue!

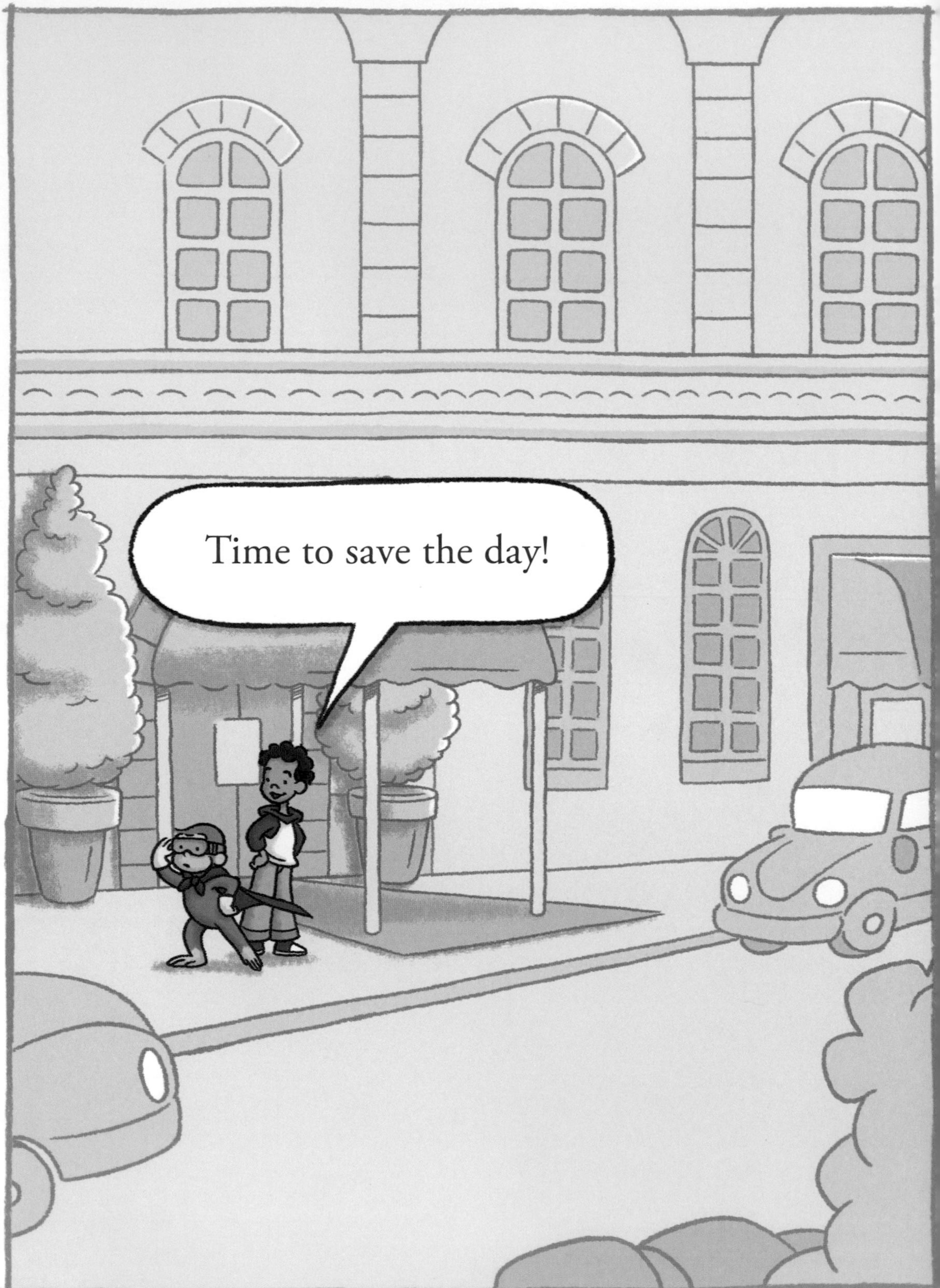
Time to save the day!

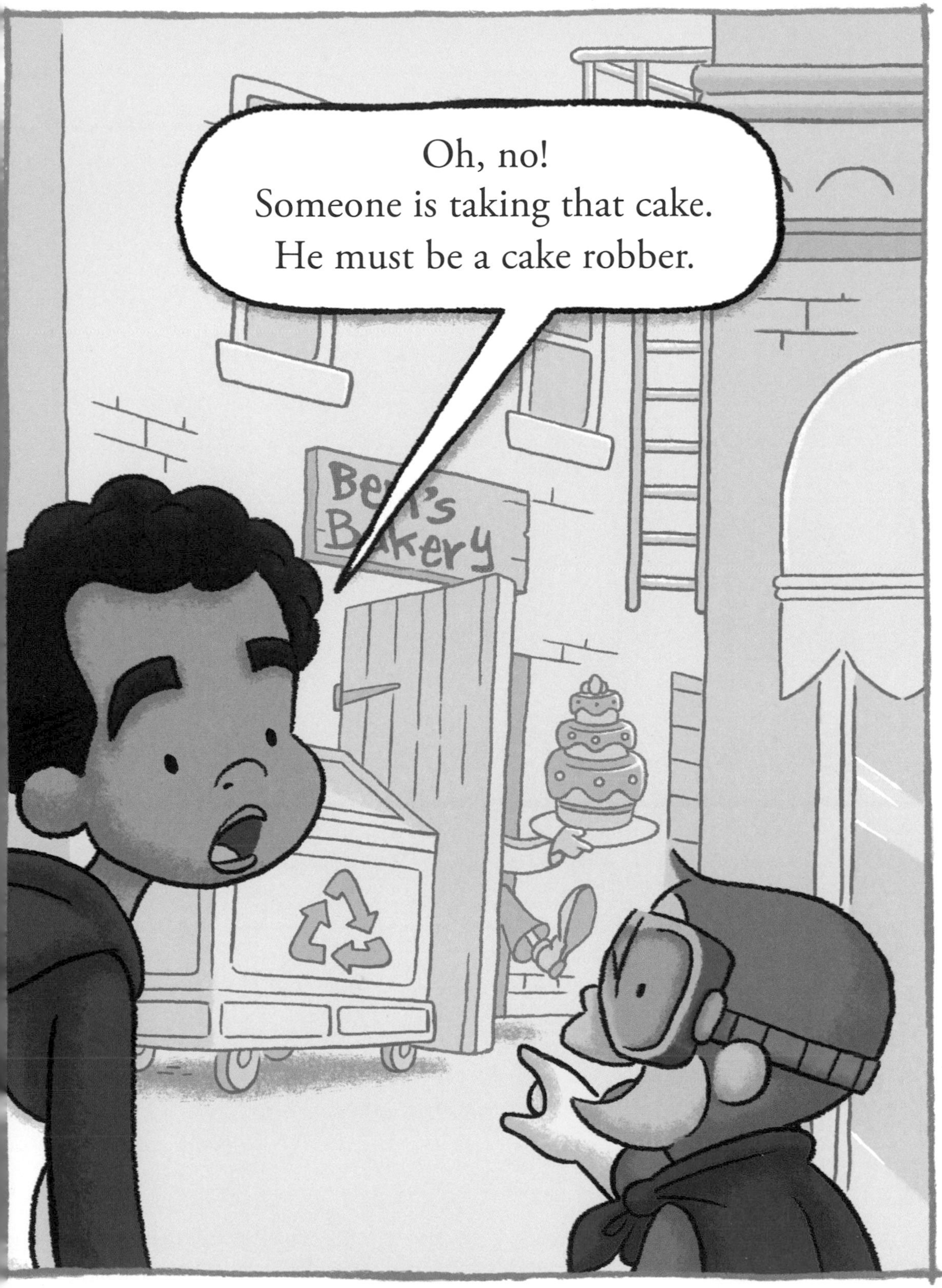
Oh, no!
Someone is taking that cake.
He must be a cake robber.

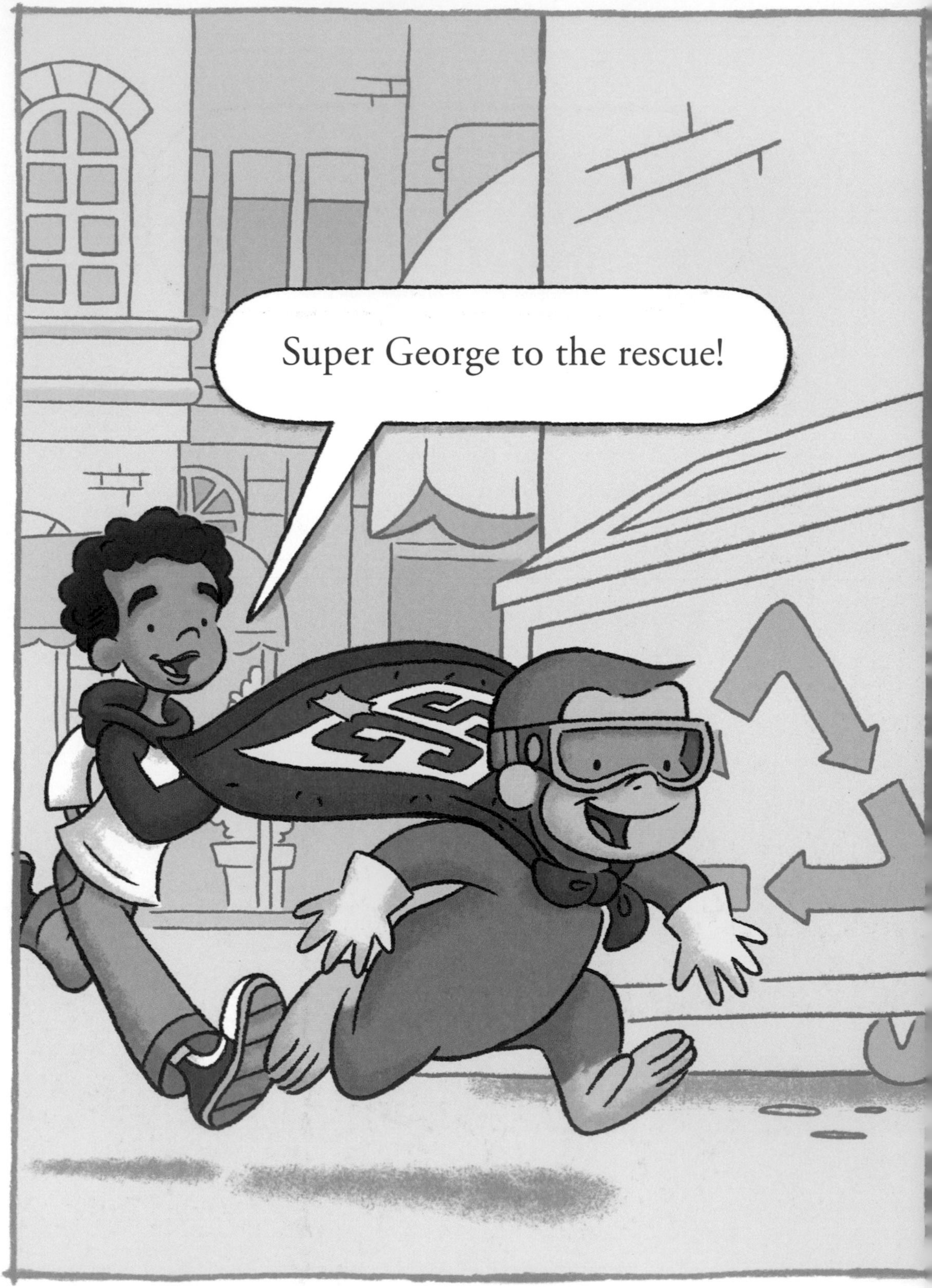
Super George to the rescue!

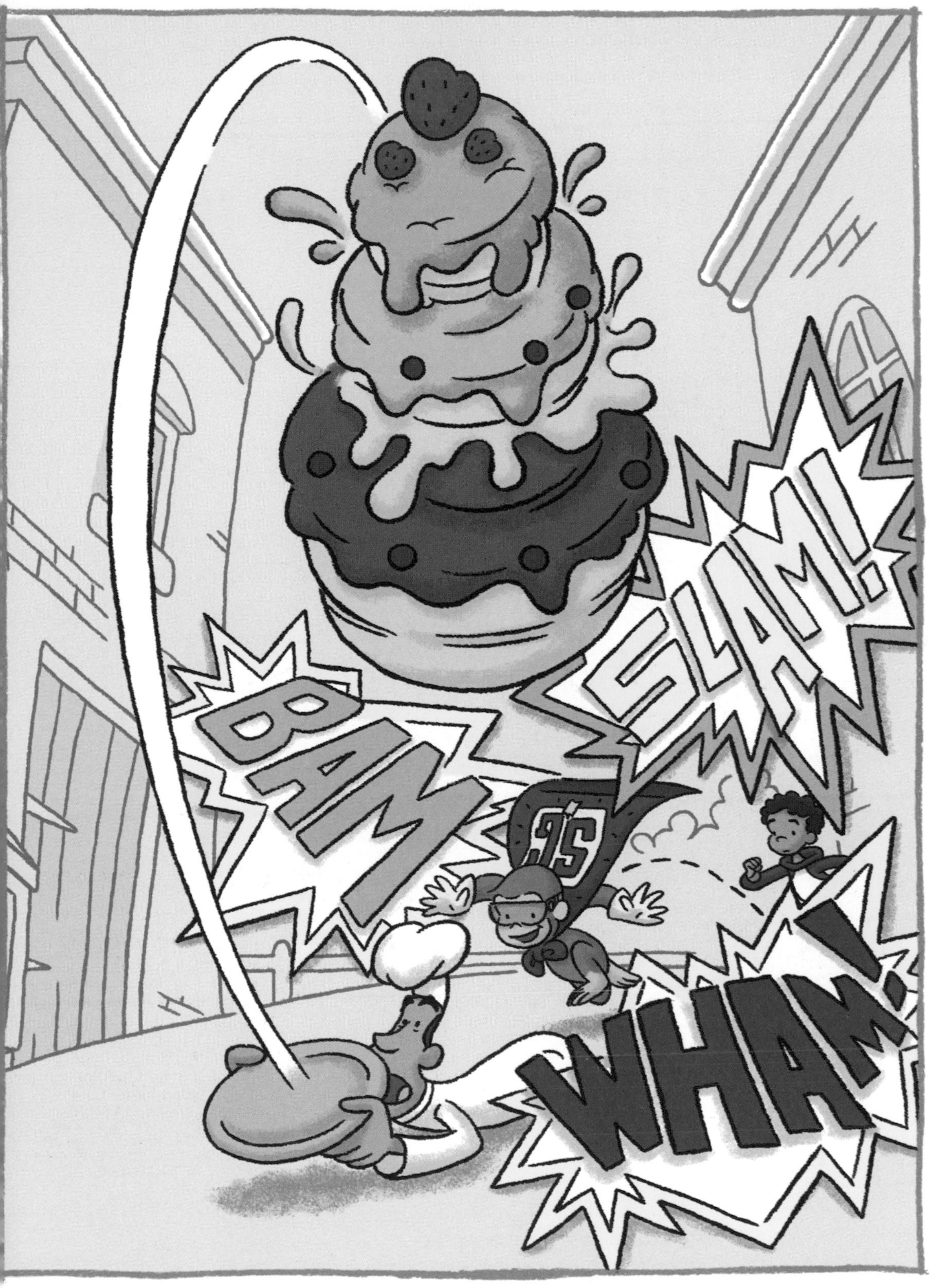
SLAM!
BAM
WHAM!

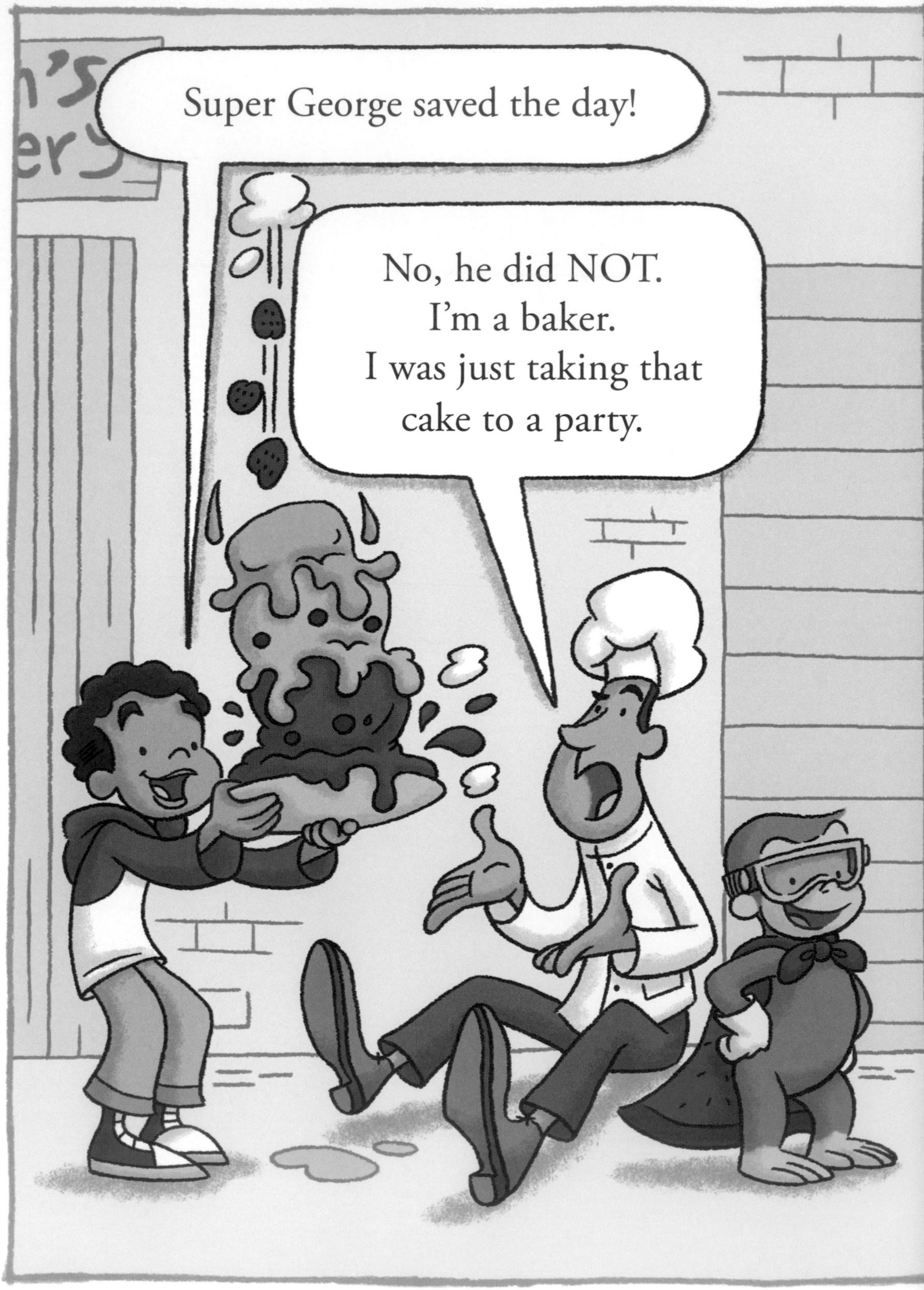
Super George saved the day!
No, he did NOT. I'm a baker. I was just taking that cake to a party.

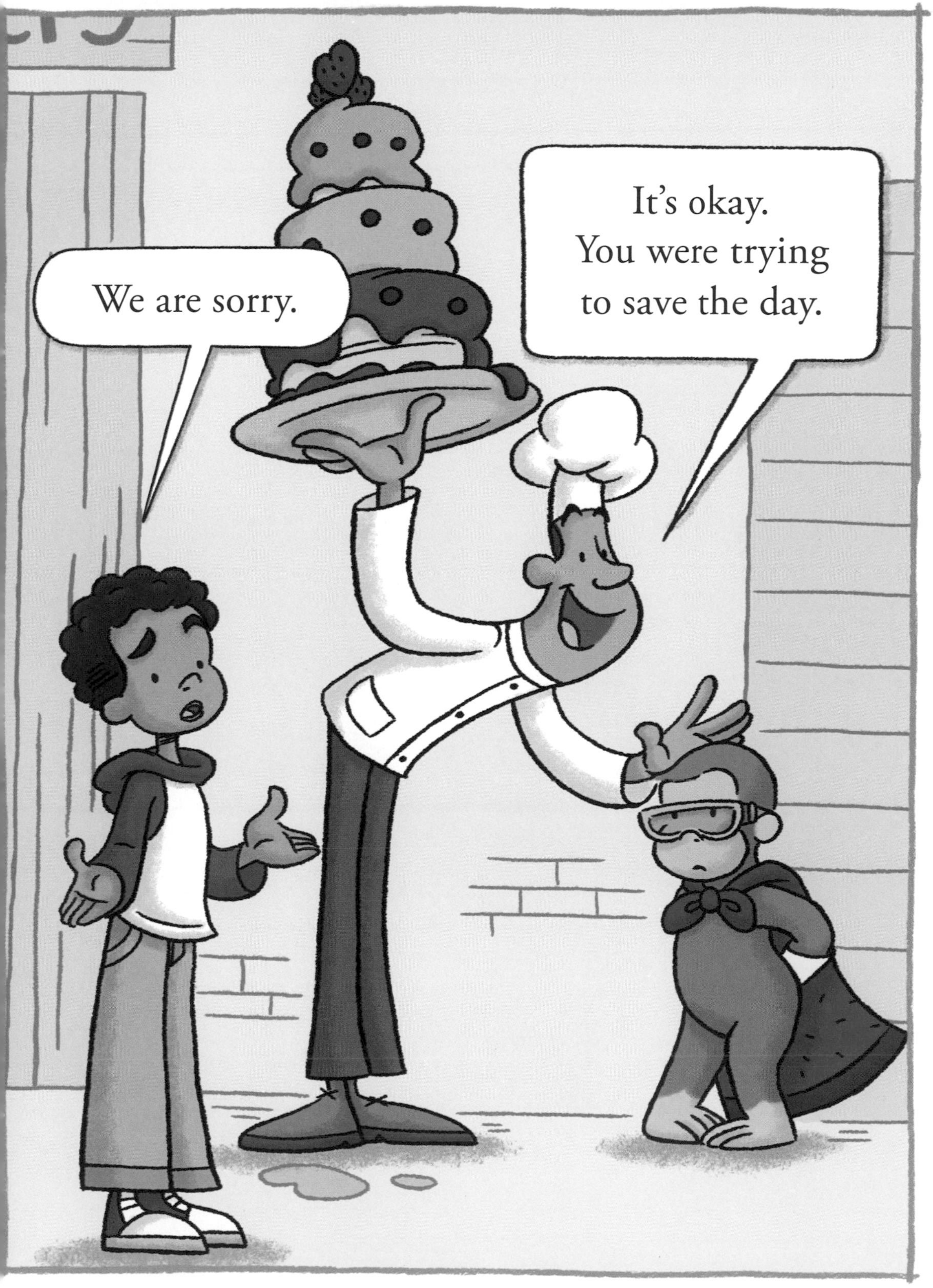
We are sorry.
It's okay. You were trying to save the day.

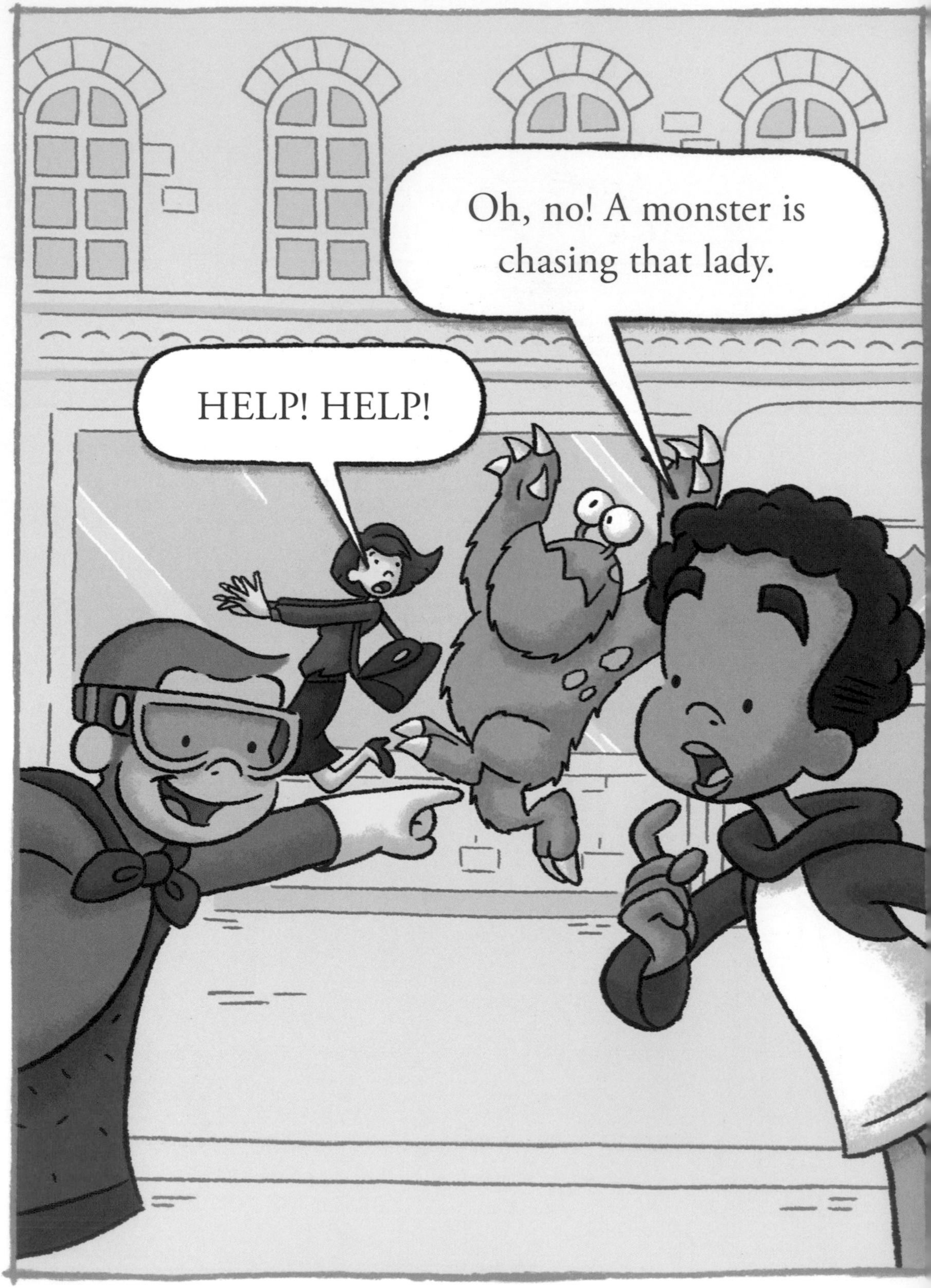
HELP! HELP!
Oh, no! A monster is chasing that lady.

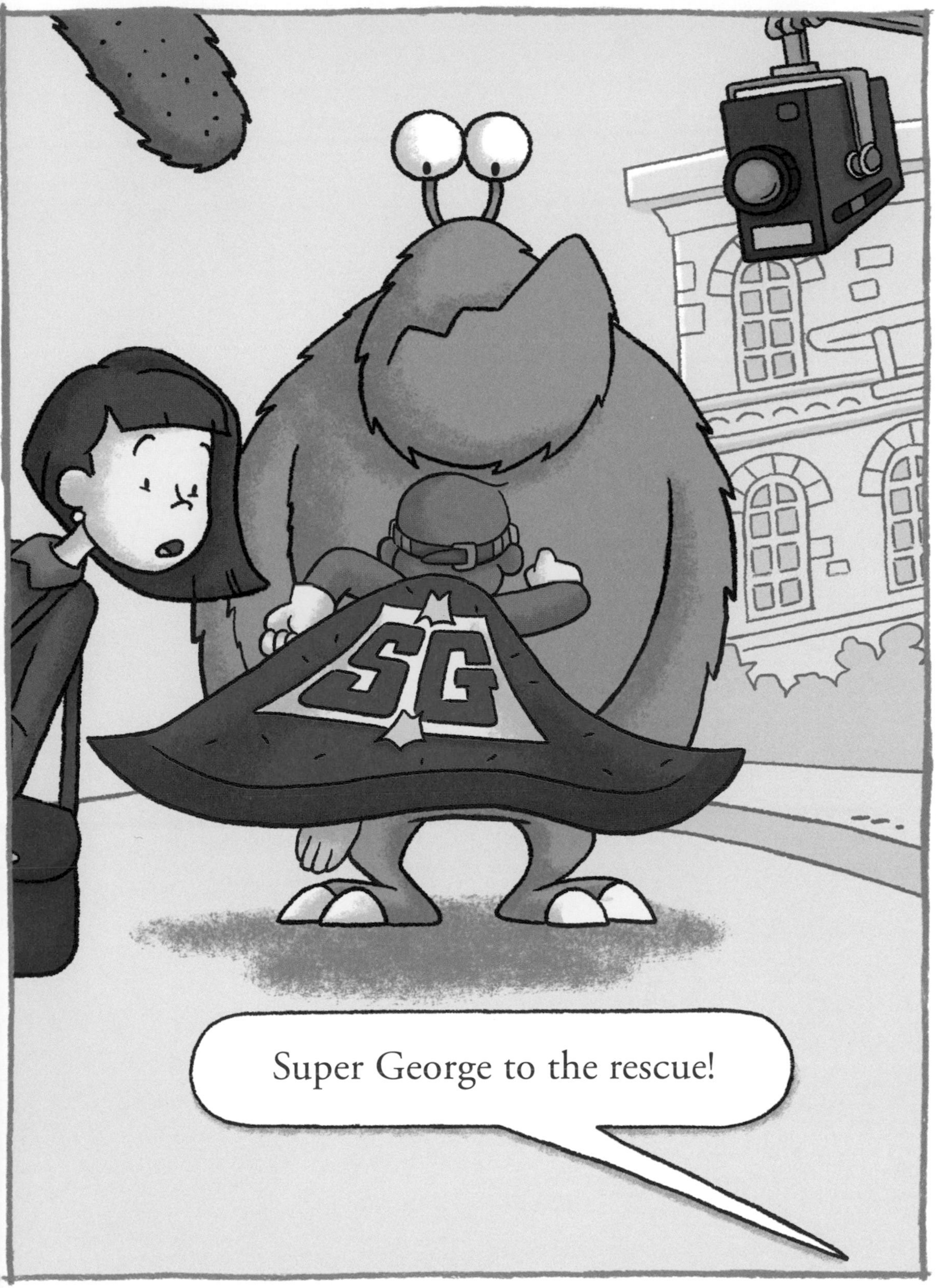
SG
Super George to the rescue!

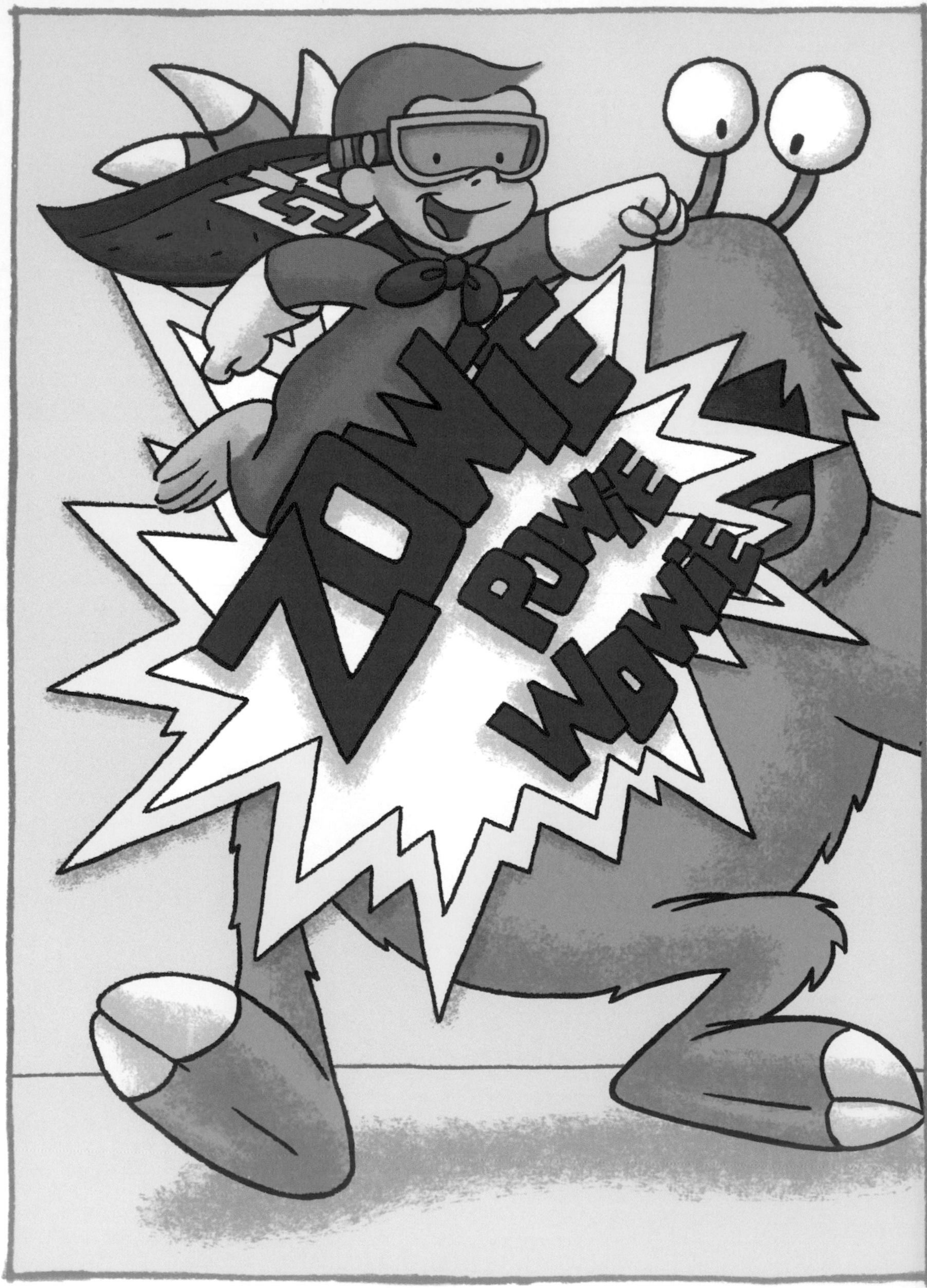
ZOWIE
POWIE
WOWIE

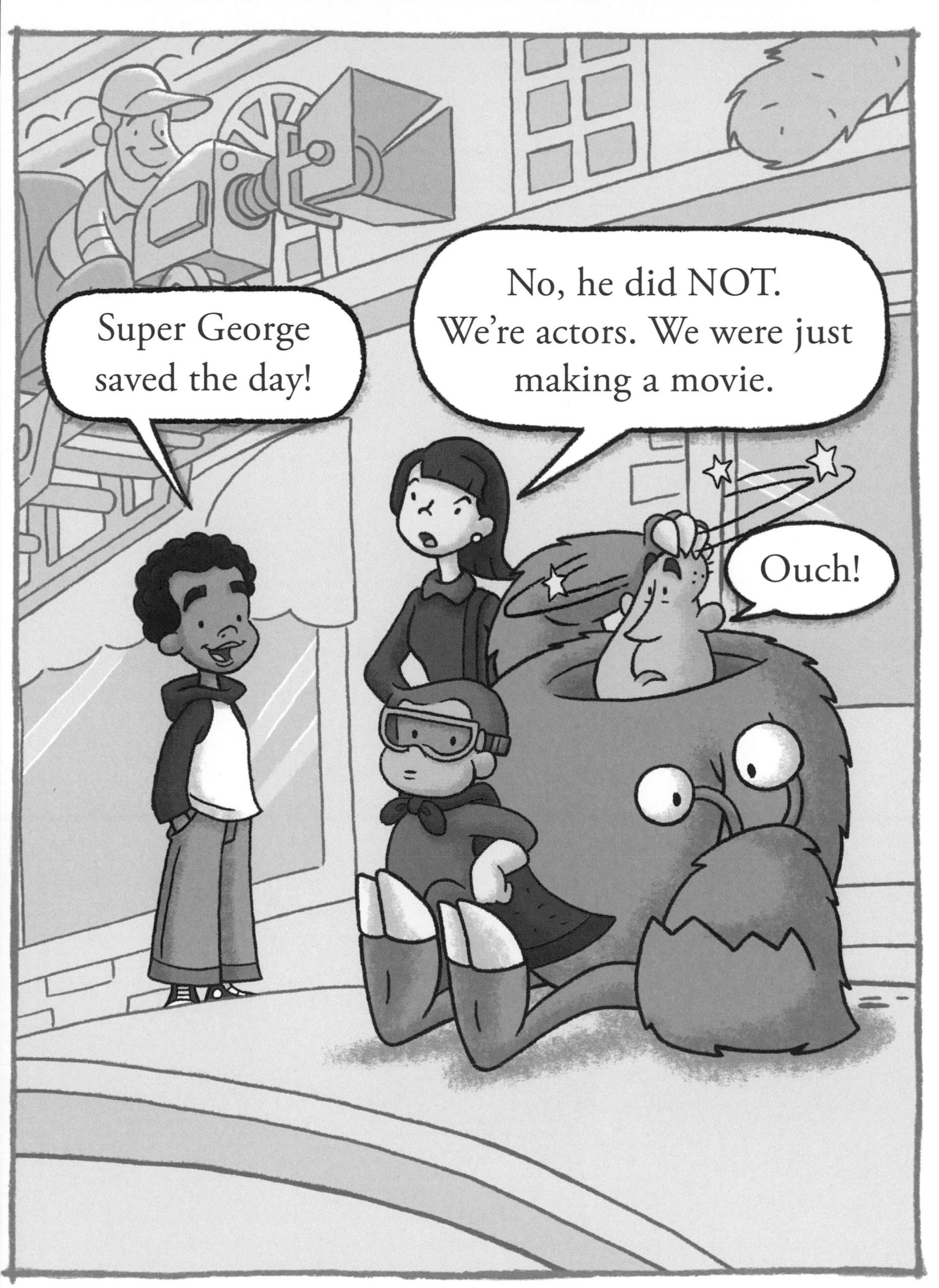
Super George saved the day!
No, he did NOT. We're actors. We were just making a movie.
Ouch!

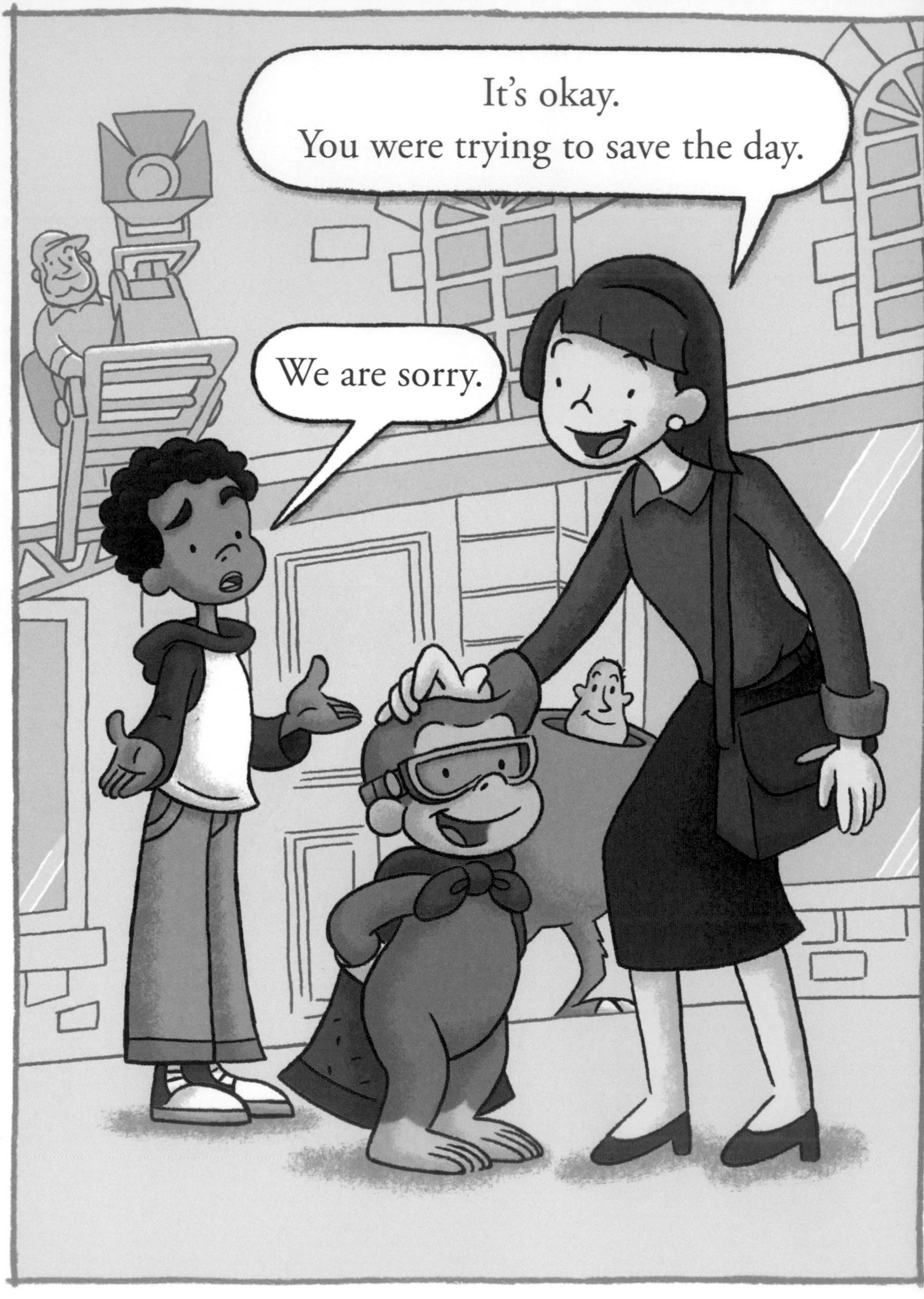
It's okay.
You were trying to save the day.
We are sorry.

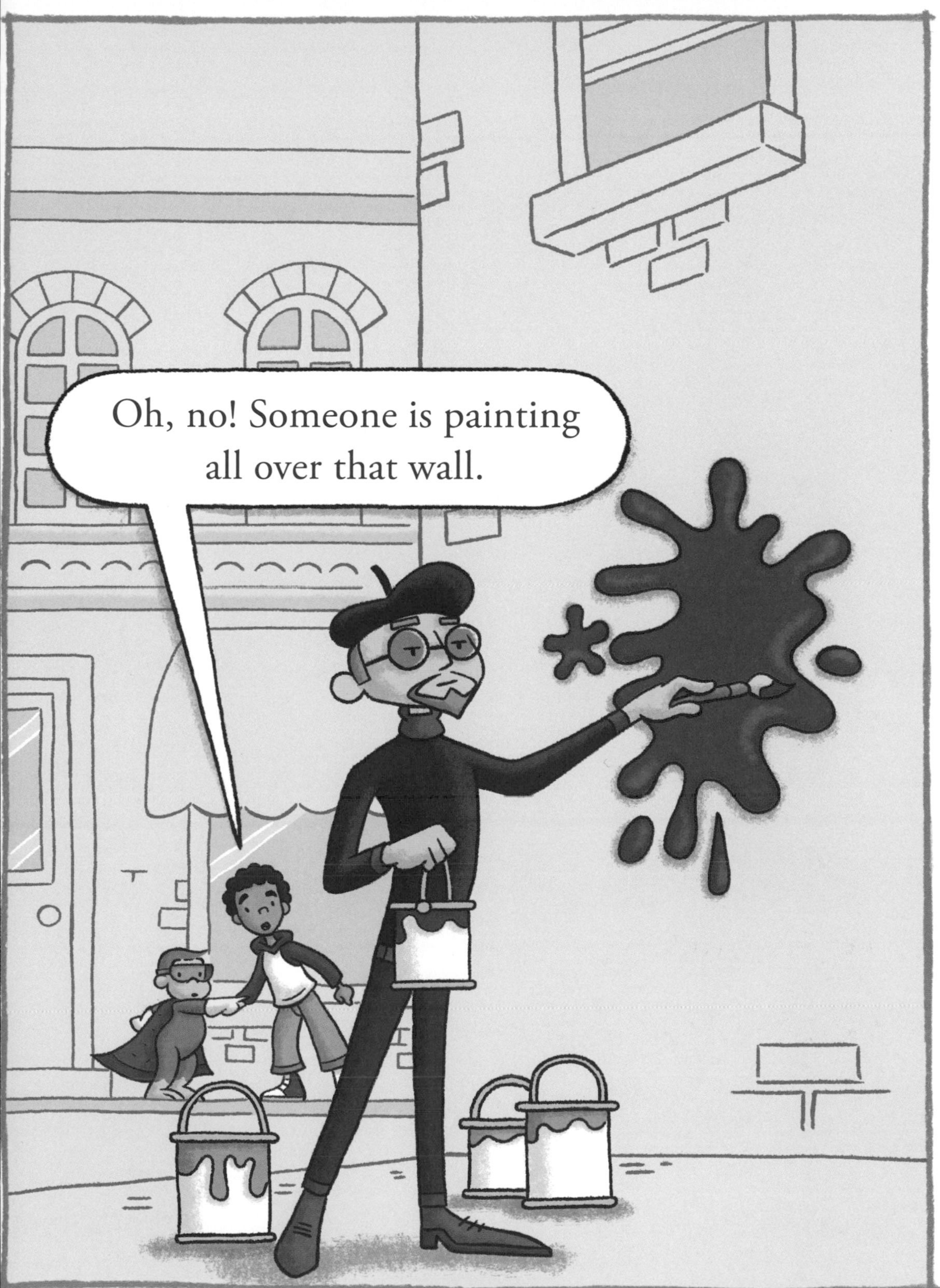
Oh, no! Someone is painting all over that wall.

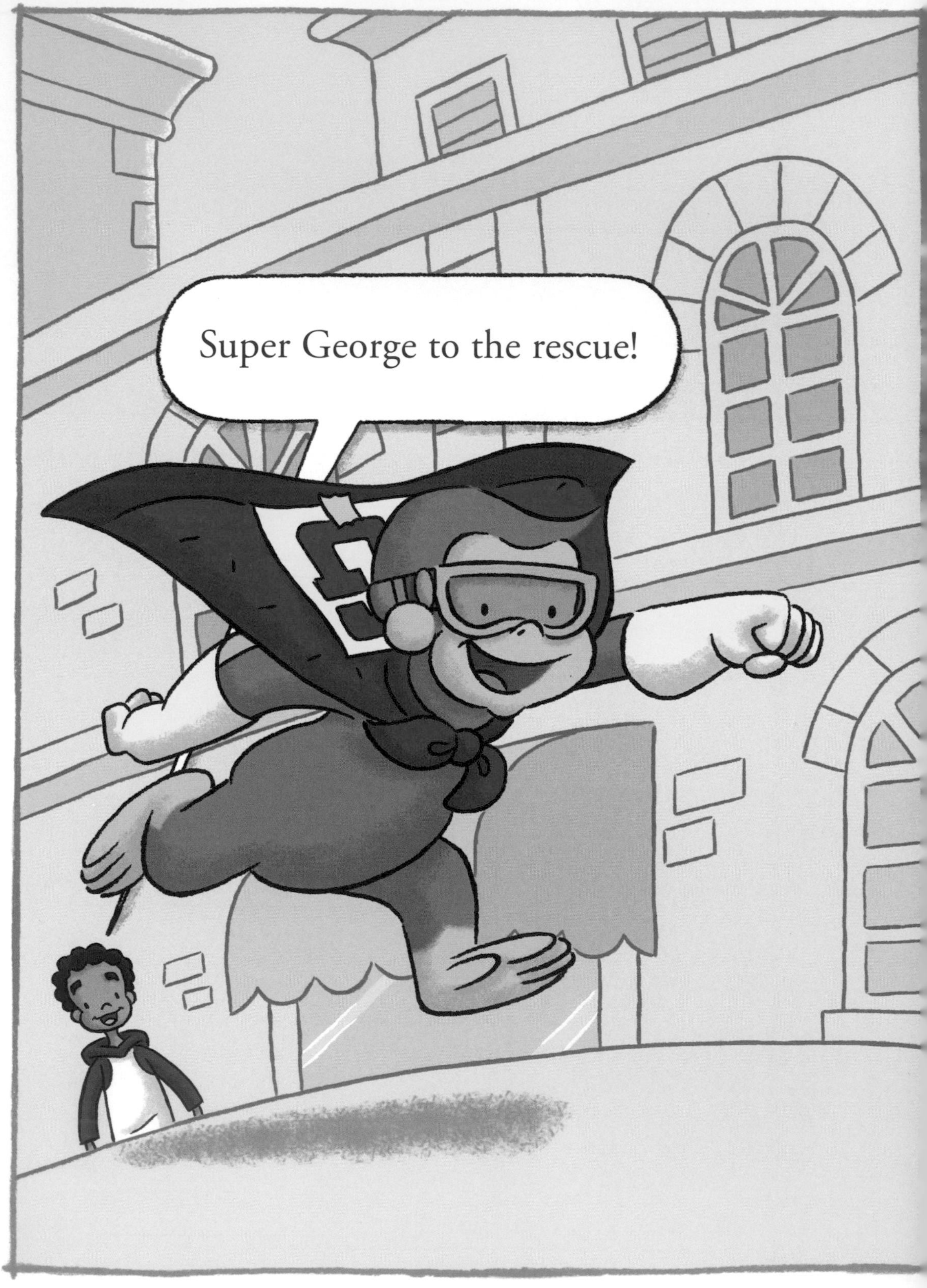
Super George to the rescue!

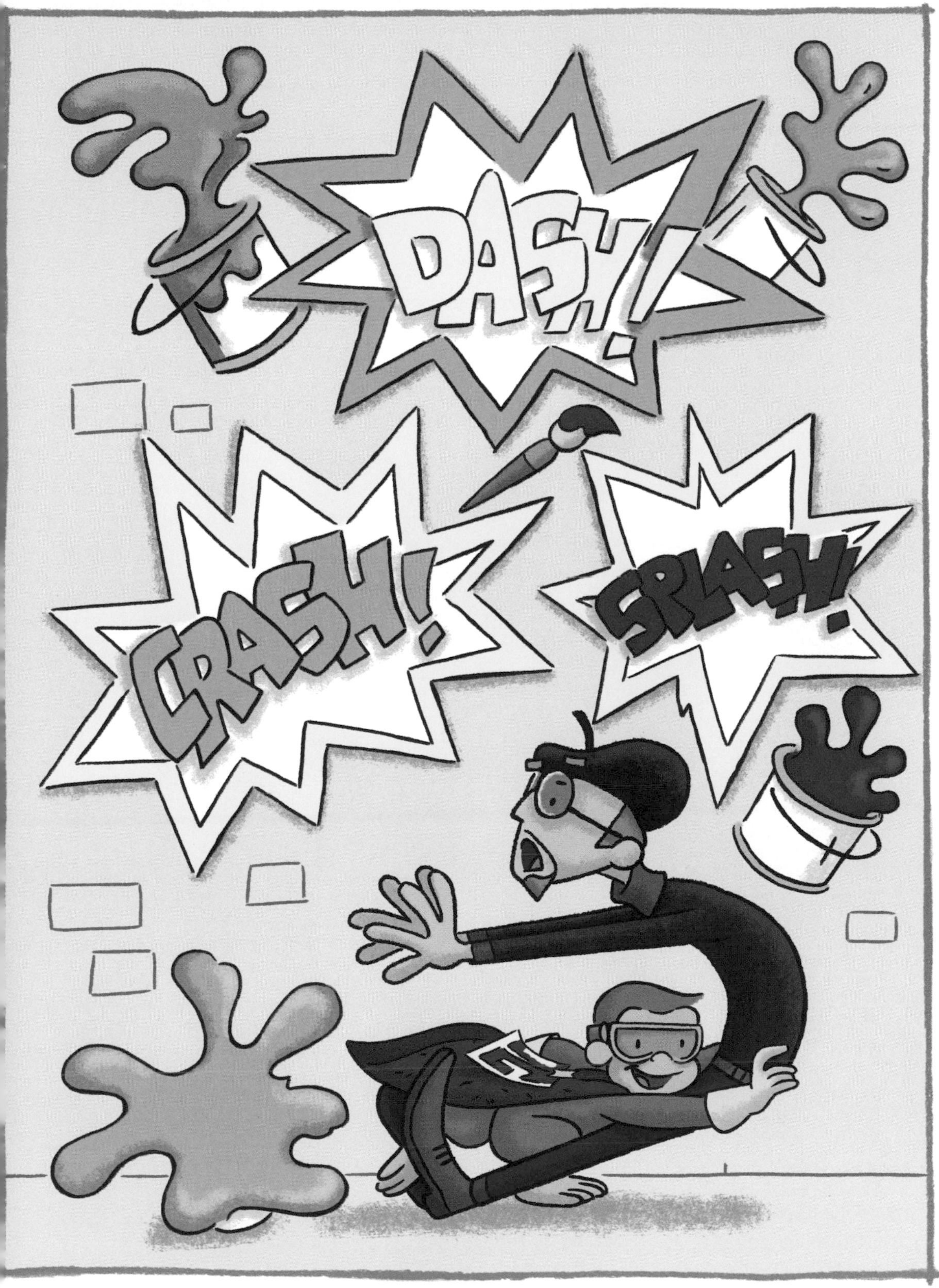
DASH!
CRASH!
SPLASH!

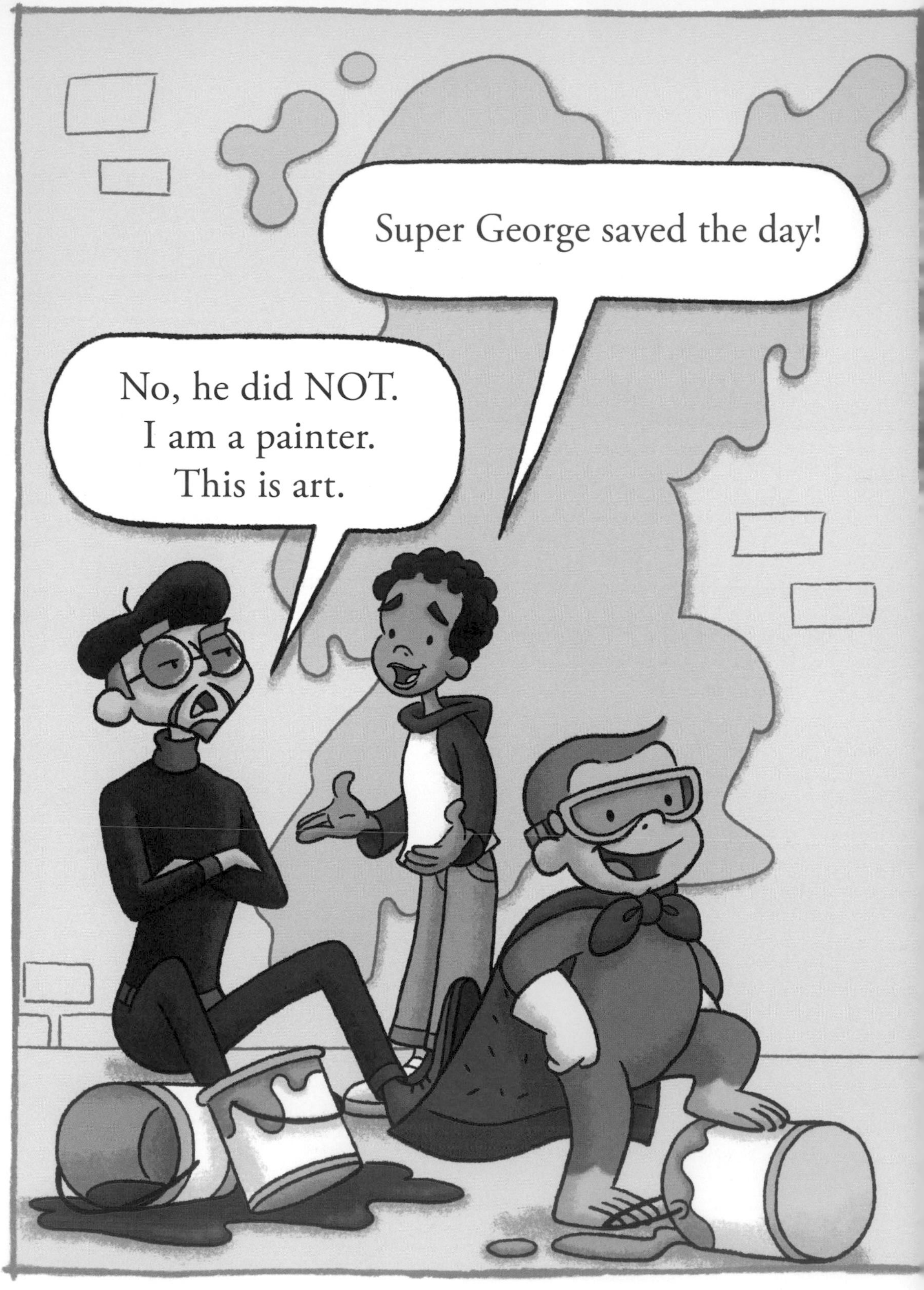
No, he did NOT.
I am a painter.
This is art.
Super George saved the day!

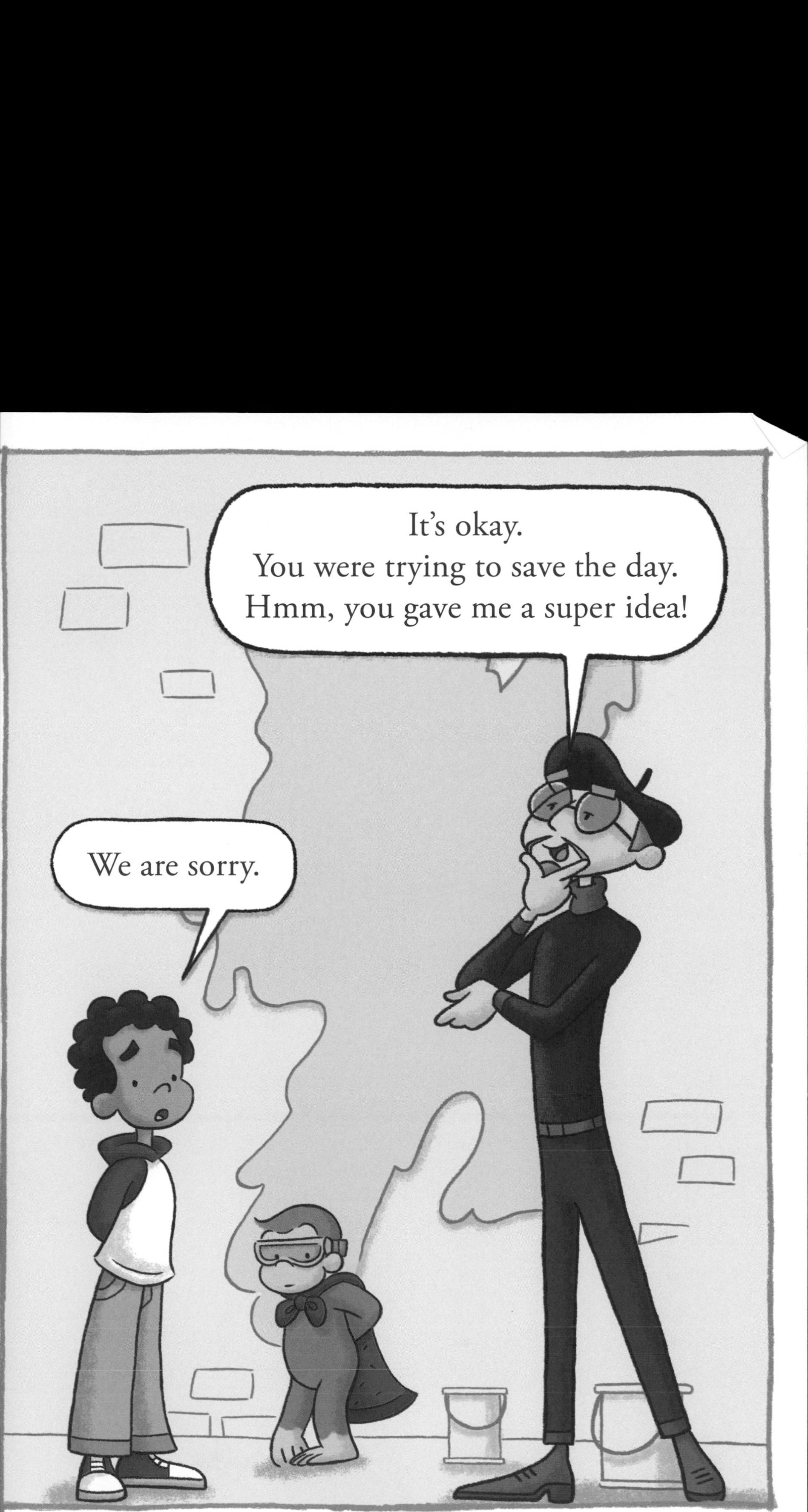
It's okay.
You were trying to save the day.
Hmm, you gave me a super idea!
We are sorry.

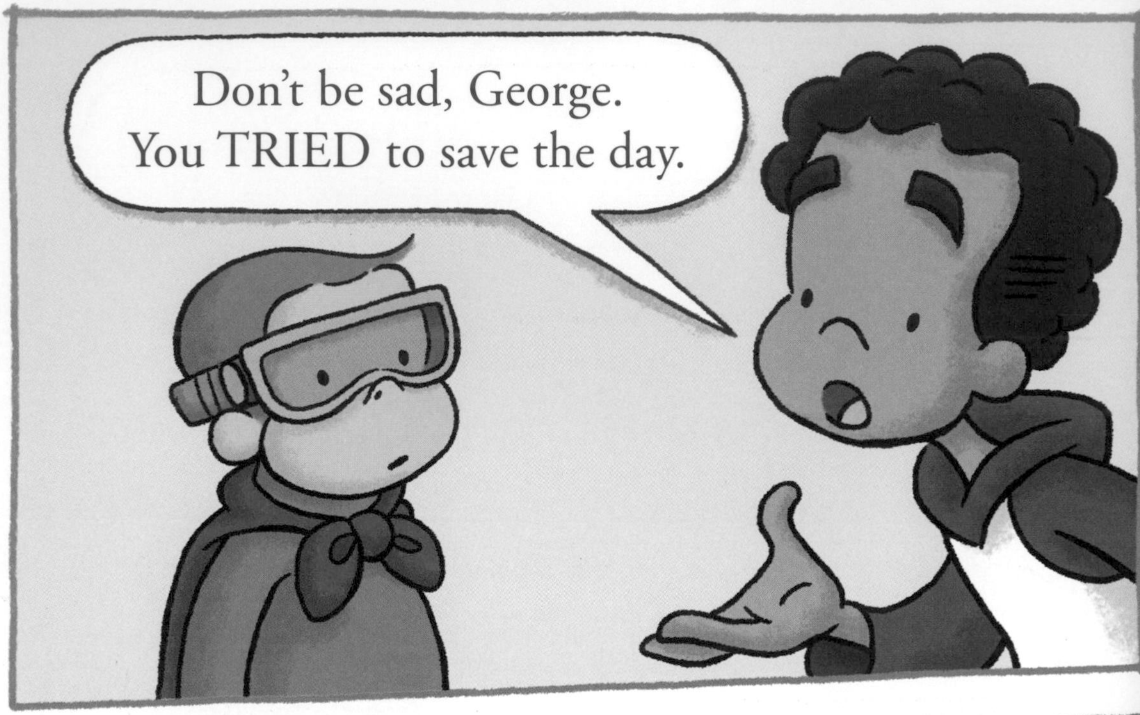
Don't be sad, George.
You TRIED to save the day.

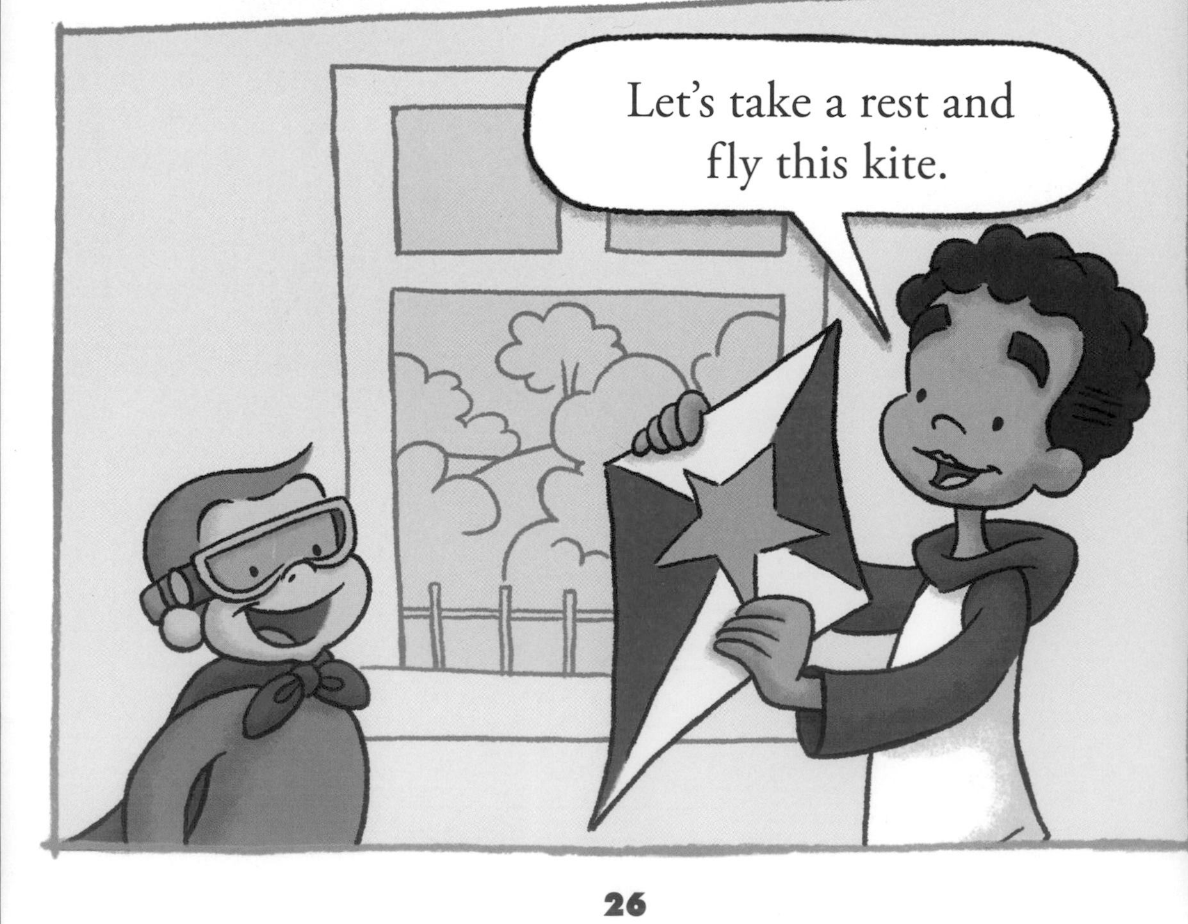
Let's take a rest and
fly this kite.

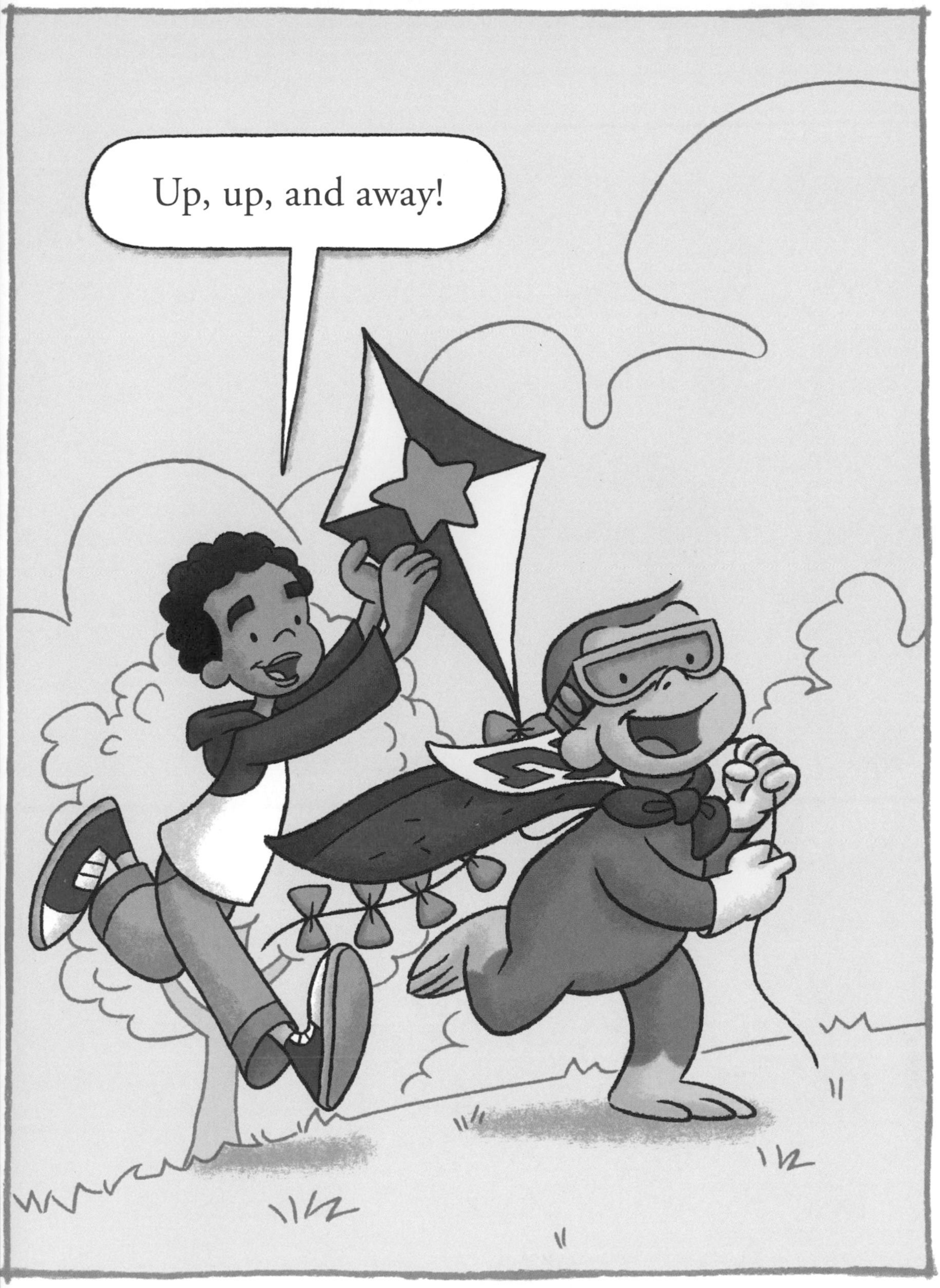
Up, up, and away!

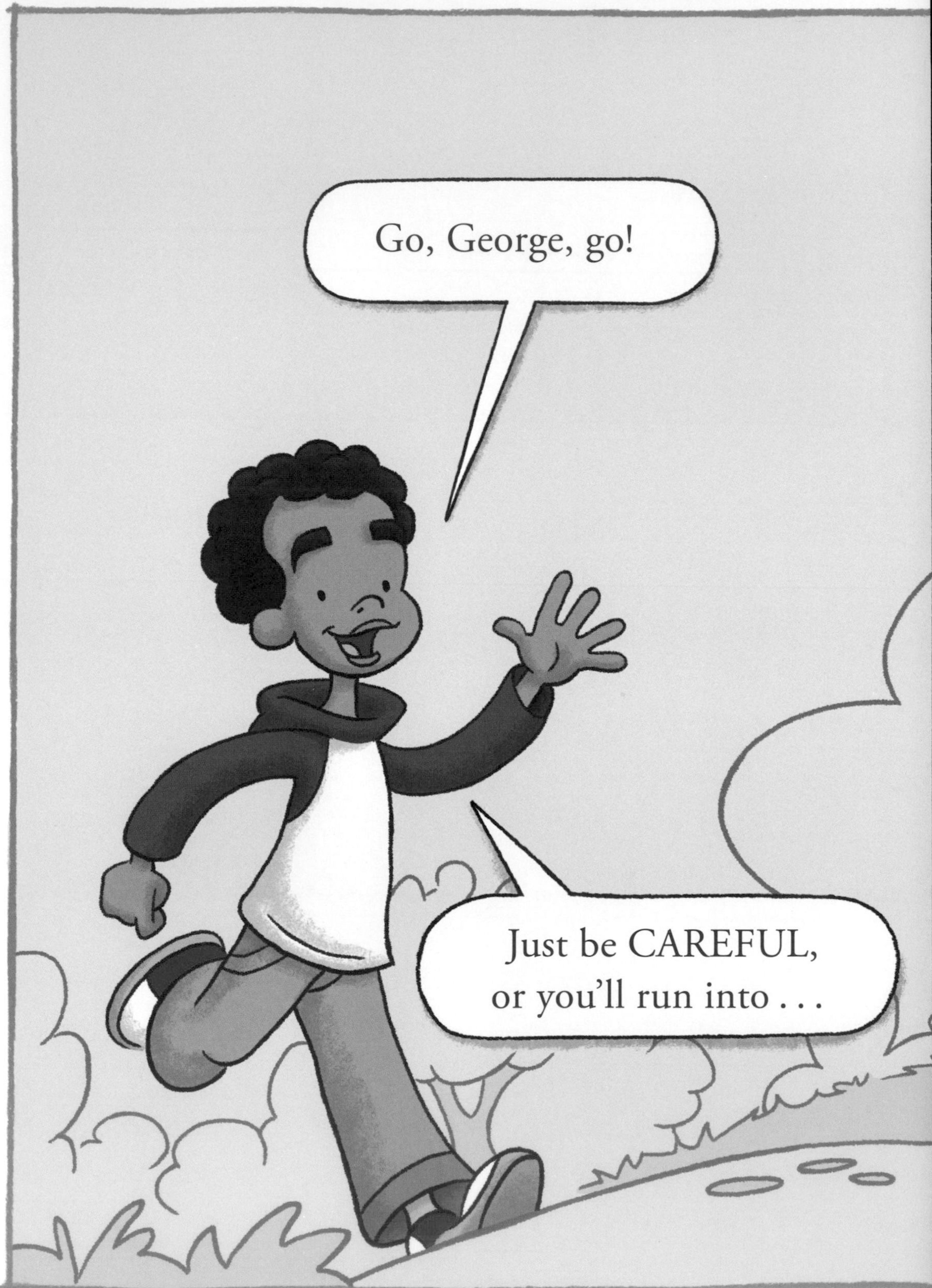
Go, George, go!
Just be CAREFUL, or you'll run into . . .

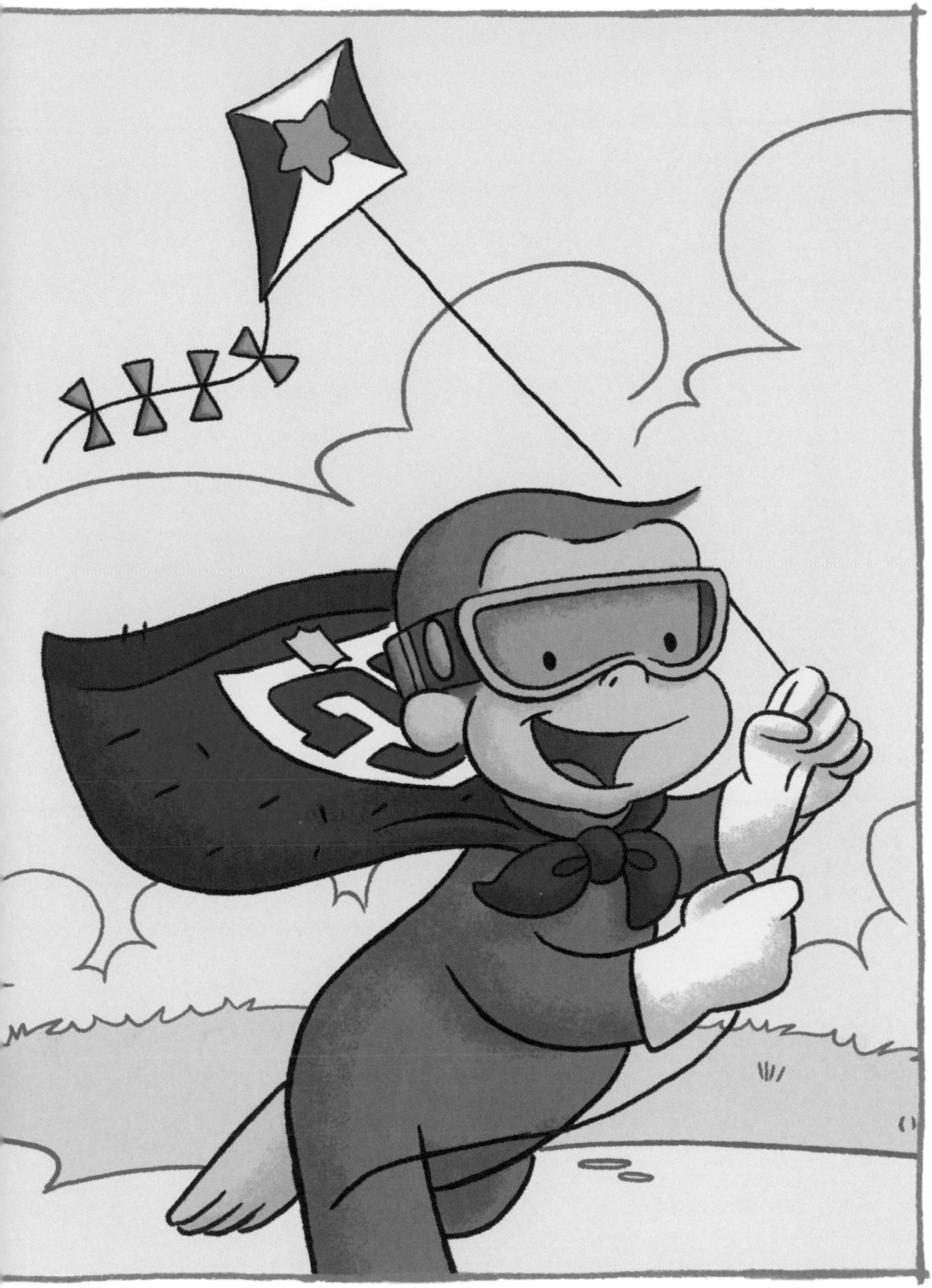

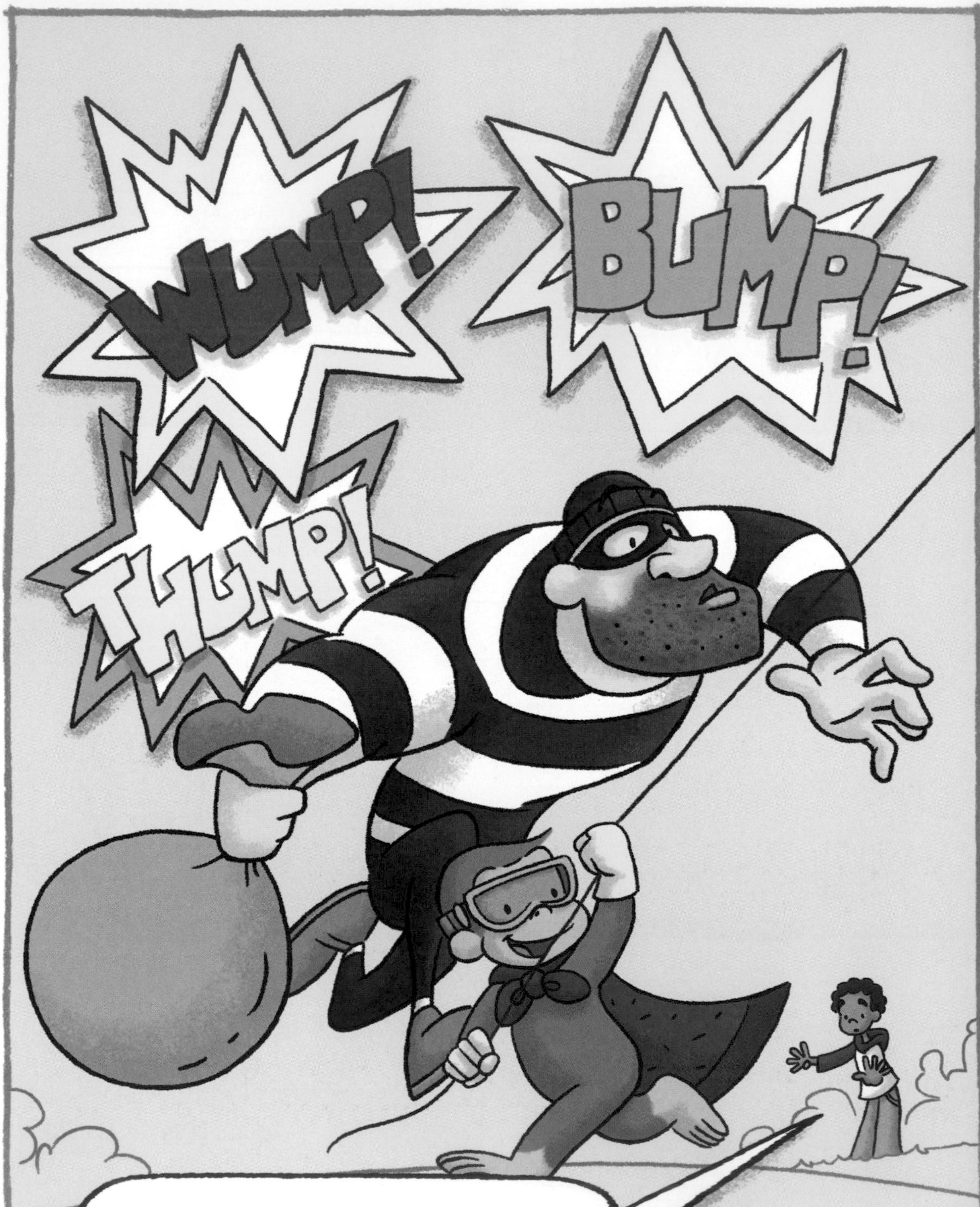
WUMP!
BUMP!
THUMP!
. . . that man with a big bag!

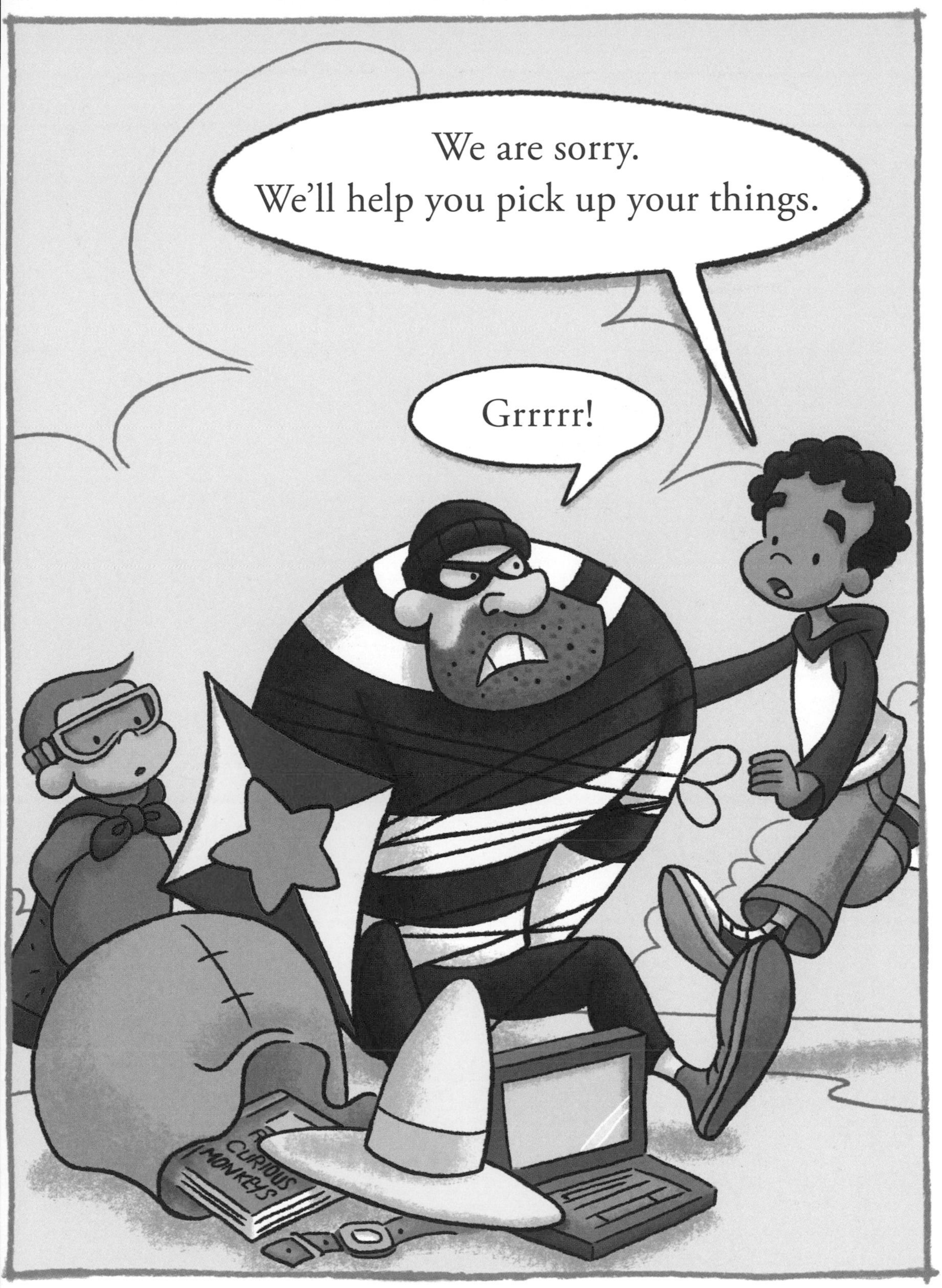
We are sorry.
We'll help you pick up your things.
Grrrrr!
FUN CURIOUS MONKEYS

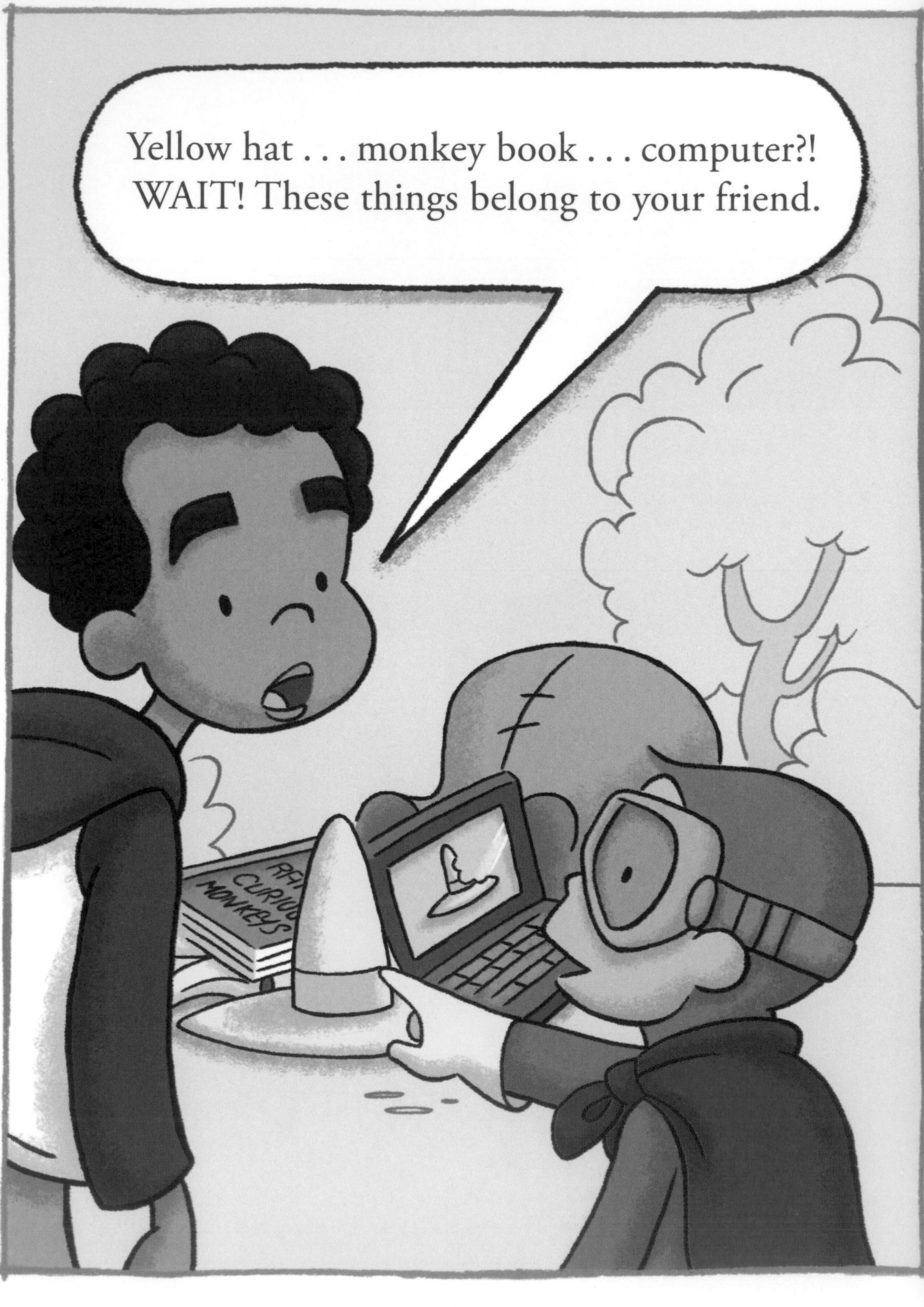
Yellow hat . . . monkey book . . . computer?! WAIT! These things belong to your friend.
MONKEYS

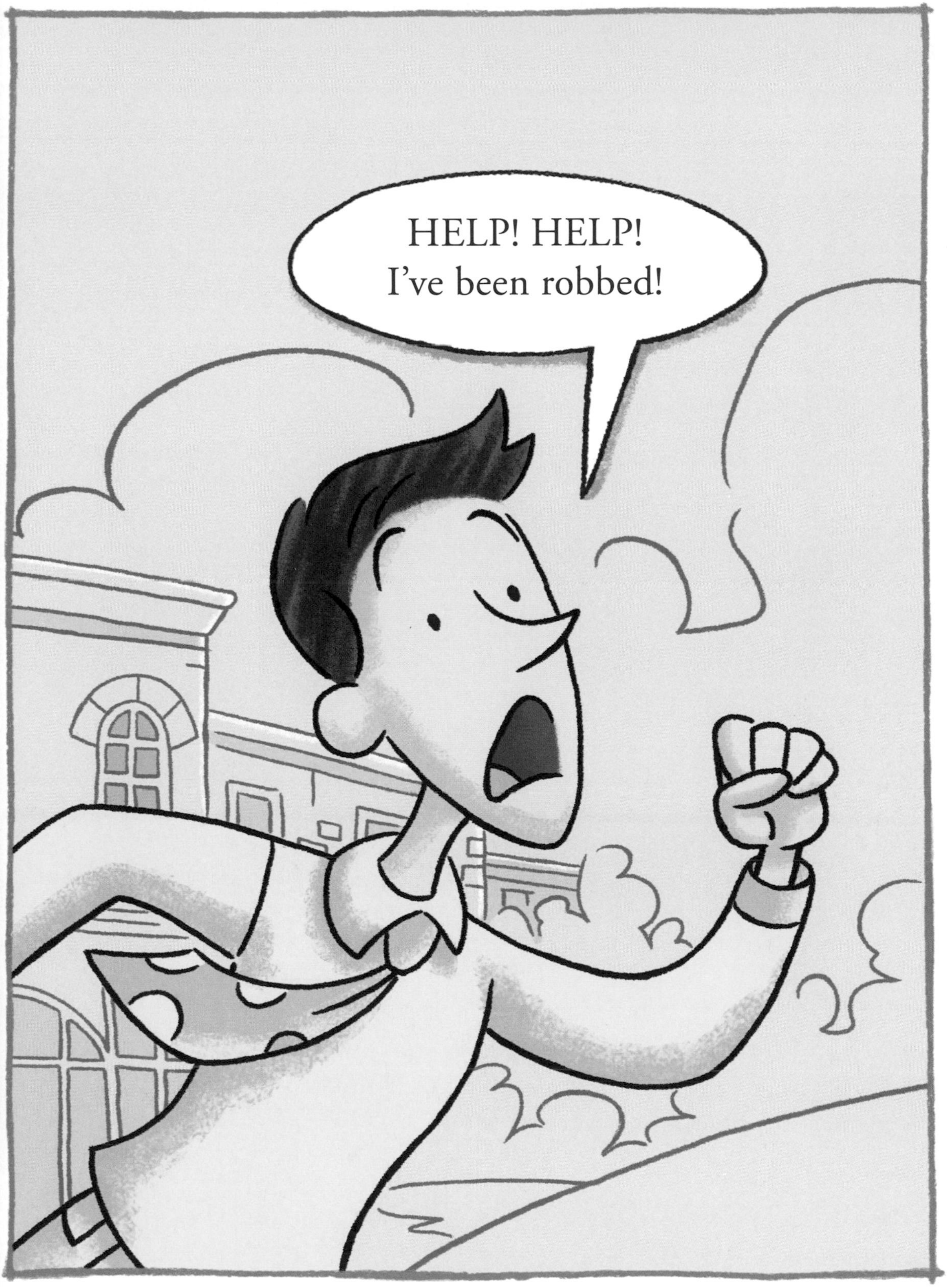
HELP! HELP!
I've been robbed!

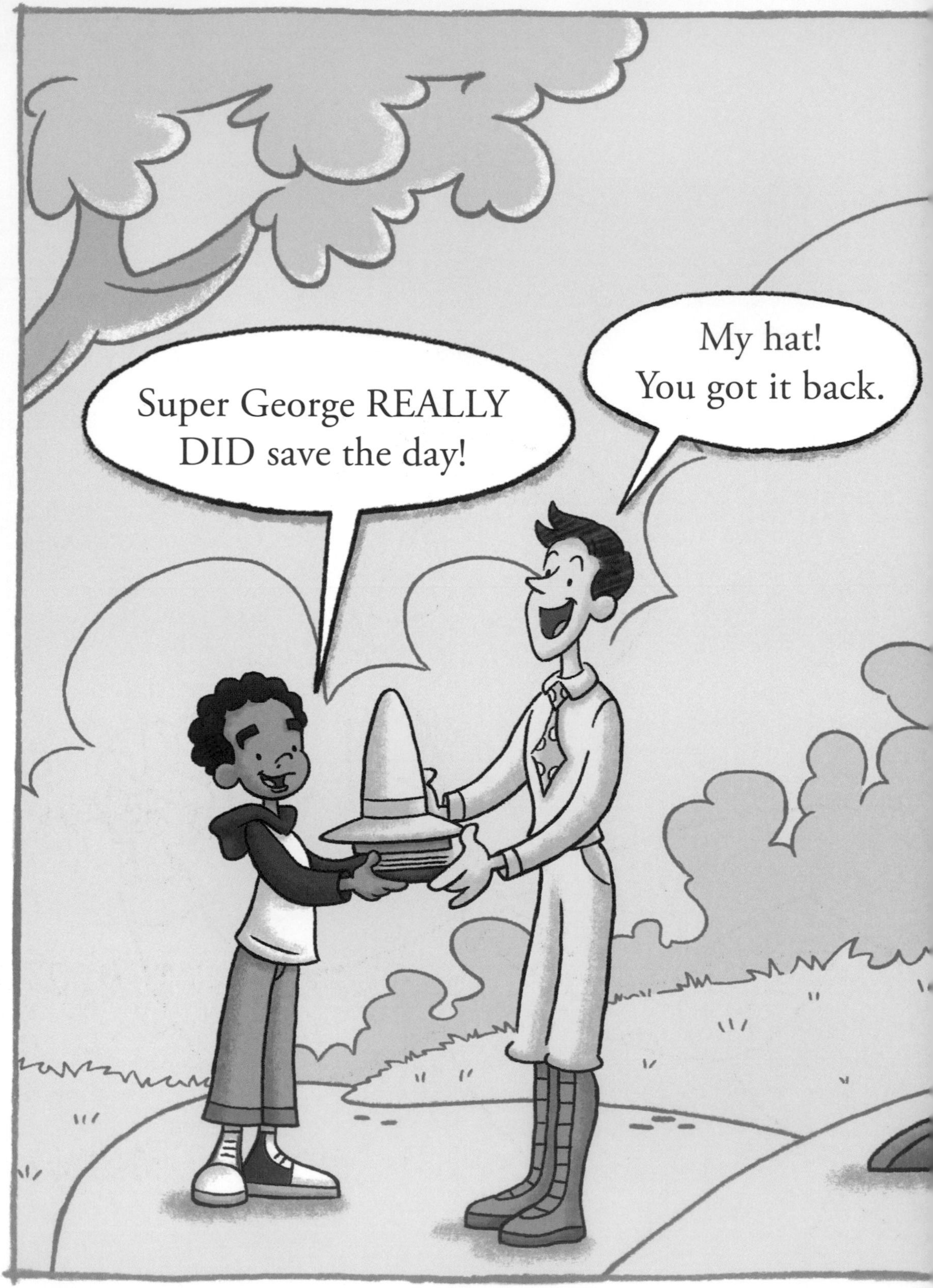
Super George REALLY DID save the day!
My hat! You got it back.

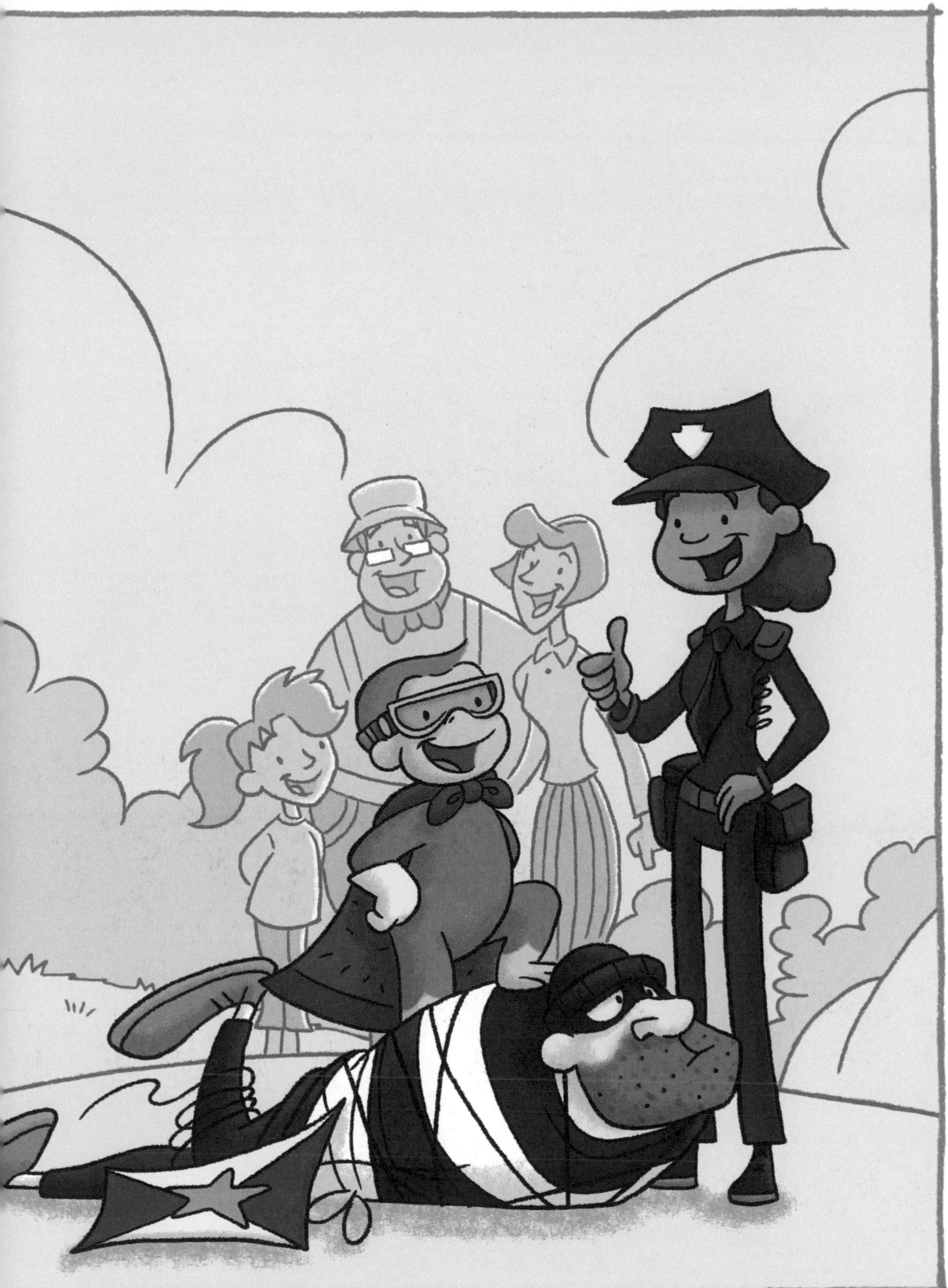

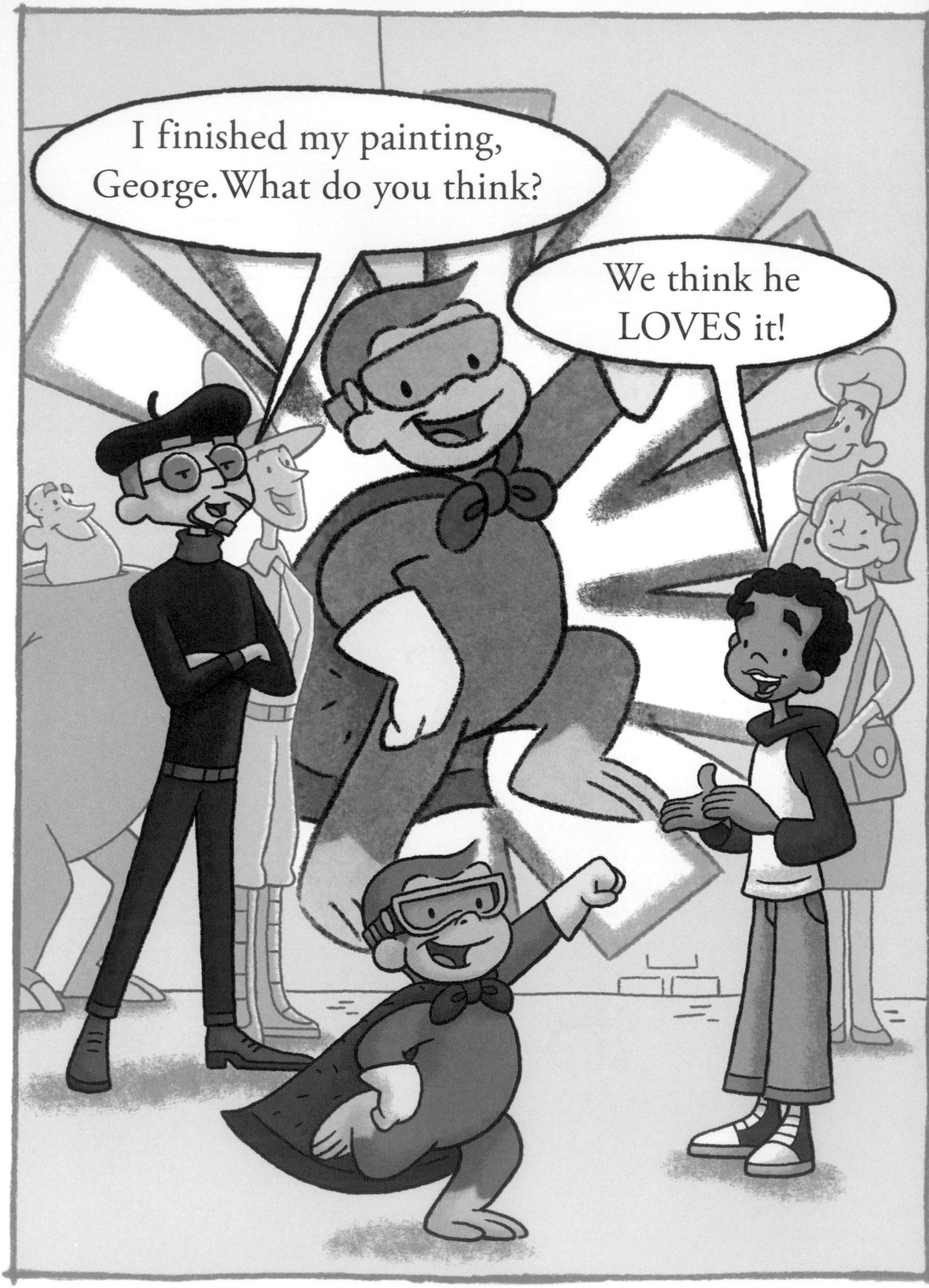
I finished my painting, George. What do you think?
We think he LOVES it!

Get your child ready to read in three simple steps!

I READ	Read the book to your child.
 **WE READ**	Read the book together.
 **YOU READ**	Encourage your child to read the book over and over again.

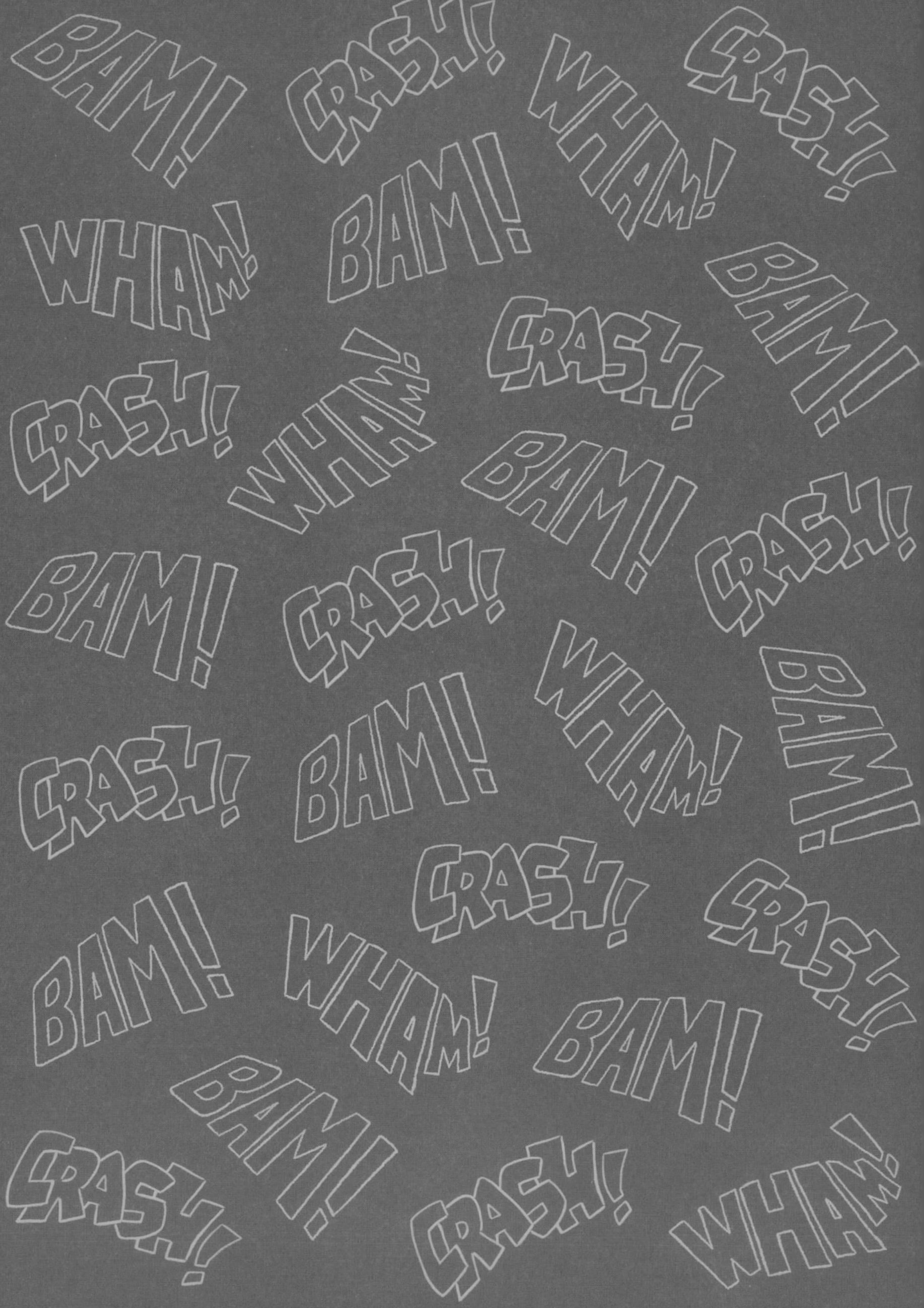
BAM!
CRASH!
WHAM!
CRASH!
BAM!
WHAM!
BAM!
CRASH!
CRASH!
WHAM!
BAM!
CRASH!
BAM!
CRASH!
WHAM!
BAM!
CRASH!
BAM!
CRASH!
CRASH!
BAM!
WHAM!
BAM!
BAM!
CRASH!
CRASH!
WHAM!